# Yɪᴘ/Tᴜᴄᴋ

This Large Print Book carries the
Seal of Approval of N.A.V.H.

# YIP/TUCK

## SPARKLE ABBEY

**THORNDIKE PRESS**

*A part of Gale, Cengage Learning*

GALE
CENGAGE Learning·

Farmington Hills, Mich • San Francisco • New York • Waterville, Maine
Meriden, Conn • Mason, Ohio • Chicago

GALE
CENGAGE Learning·

LIBRARY OF CONGRESS CATALOGING-IN-PUBLICATION DATA

Abbey, Sparkle.
    Yip/tuck / by Sparkle Abbey. — Large Print edition.
        pages cm. — (A Pampered Pets Mysteries series ; Book 4) (Thorndike Press Large Print Clean Reads)
    ISBN-13: 978-1-4104-6743-0 (hardcover)
    ISBN-10: 1-4104-6743-0 (hardcover)
    1. Pet grooming salons—Fiction. 2. Pet owners—Fiction. 3. Murder—Investigation—Fiction. 4. Laguna Beach (Calif.)—Fiction. 5. Large type books. I. Title.
PS3601.B359Y57 2014
813'.6—dc23                                                    2013047777

Published in 2014 by arrangement with BelleBooks, Inc.

Printed in Mexico
1 2 3 4 5 6 7 18 17 16 15 14

To Matisse, Abby, Cinder, Callie, Nemo, Kokomo, and all our other four-legged furry loved ones who have crossed the Rainbow Bridge. You'll forever be in our hearts.

# CHAPTER ONE

"Have you worked in retail before, Vera?"

Vera White, a fifty-something with steel-wool hair, sat ramrod straight, palms flat on her denim leggings.

"No." Her thin lips flashed a skittish smile.

I waited for more details but none came. She reminded me of an overweight Yorkie at a six-year-old's birthday party — a cute bundle of nerves ready to attack at the slightest provocation.

I shifted in my chair and pretended to review her application, hoping she'd elaborate. "Pretended" because there wasn't much to read. Other than her current personal information, the form was blank — no job history, no skills, no references. Nothing to give me an idea if she was equipped to handle Bow Wow's unique clientele — the pampered pooches of Laguna Beach. Trust me, there were a lot them.

"So, why do you think you'd like to work here?" I asked. Her hands fisted and then relaxed. "I've been in hypnotherapy for a year now. My therapist said I should consider a part-time job. I saw your Help Wanted sign last week." She spoke slowly, as if she'd memorized her answers. Probably coached by her therapist.

Her gaze darted over my shoulder toward the checkout counter, then back at me. "I've researched you."

Great. I could only imagine what she'd found. Melinda Langston, owner of Bow Wow Boutique, was a former Miss America contestant, disqualified in a humiliating scandal. Melinda Langston, runaway fiancée of local art gallery owner. Melinda Langston, recently "helped" Laguna Beach police find local drama queen's killer.

"Your shop is clean." Her tone was matter-of-fact, but her gaze roamed the store like a Nervous Nelly.

Obviously, her answer wasn't the direction I thought she was going. However, I was happy to hear Bow Wow had a respectable reputation. I'd worked hard to make my pet boutique a success.

"Although," she continued, "I don't think you should allow animals inside. Do you know how many germs and diseases they carry?" She shuddered then looked at the counter again.

I couldn't stop myself. I looked over my shoulder. I scanned the room quickly, trying to see it from her point of view. A variety of collars, leads, carriers, beds, toys, specialty items, and apparel, the locked glass counter was free of clutter and fingerprints.

Momentary panic gripped me. Had I left the cash register drawer out? Nope. I faced Wacky Vera. I had no idea what had grabbed her peculiar interest.

"I don't see any antibacterial hand sanitizer, but that's okay. I have my own until you buy some," she said. "You're wearing jeans and a T-shirt. Is that the dress code, or would I have to wear a uniform? I must wear my own clothing. No polyester. I have a doctor's note." She opened her black leather handbag. Head down, she pulled out three small bottles of hand sanitizer, a signed document, which I assumed was her release from communal polyester, and a sealed sandwich baggie containing a pair of purple exam gloves.

"You carry disposable gloves?" I suddenly understood the lack of work experience. I opened my mouth, planning to end the interview, but she continued before I could get the words out.

"Of course. I never know when I might need them. I'm allergic to latex. Horrible hives, itching, wheezing, difficulty breathing. You'd have to carry a non-latex brand just for me. I use a minimum of one box each month."

She must have mistaken my look of frozen engrossment for confusion.

"When you clean, you wear protective gloves, don't you? It's not just about the bacteria carried by the animals, but the people, too." She gasped, eyes bulging. "You clean up after them, right? Humans and animals? Do you have bleach? Hot water?" Her voice squeaked in alarm.

I didn't use anything more than a doo-doo bag, disinfectant spray, and a mop, but I didn't think she could handle the truth. I should have known this was going to be a bust when she'd opened the door with a disposable hand wipe and refused to shake hands.

I cleared my throat. A strand of hair fell from my ponytail. I tucked it behind my ear. "I really appreciate that you'd like to work here, but I'm not sure this is a good fit for you. Have you thought about one of the smaller boutiques downtown? There are a number of clothing stores looking for help."

She recoiled. "No. I can't pick up any item someone else has worn, however briefly. I can't touch someone else's food. Oh, and I cannot handle money. I have a doctor's note for all of that, too."

I'm sure she did. I wondered how many "doctor's notes" she had in her magical bag. "This job would require you to handle money."

She wrinkled her nose. "Your customers are rich. Don't they pay with credit cards?"

There was something endearing about Wacky Vera's obvious phobia, but there was no way I was hiring her.

"I'm really sorry, but I don't think you'll enjoy working here."

Agitated, she wiggled in her chair. "I know what you're thinking. You think that because I-I don't like touching people, and I-I can't handle germs, I won't be an excellent worker. Well, you're wrong. What about Monk? I've seen every episode. He had many more issues than I do. If Monk could work with the police, dirty suspects, and dead people, I can work here. With you." She tugged the hem of her tunic sweater. Her round face had flushed in her passionate outrage.

"Monk's a fictional character from a

television show that went off the air years ago."

Her dark brown eyes bulged in indignation. "And?"

Yikes. Thankfully, the phone rang, and I didn't have to come up with a polite response. I excused myself.

"Bow Wow Boutique, this is Mel."

"Jack O'Doggle," the voice on the other end said.

"Hey, Dr. O. What can I do for you?"

Dr. Jack O'Doggle, plastic surgeon to the rich and richer of Orange County, was hot. I'm not talking temperature. Tall, dark-haired, and charismatic. Let's just say he represented his profession very, very well. He was also Tova Randall's boyfriend.

For those of you who don't know, Tova and I don't play well together. Mostly because she tried to sue me for giving her pup, Kiki, fleas. I hadn't, but at the time, Tova didn't believe me.

Ever since Jack and Tova hooked up, Tova's been in my hair constantly. Dr. O seemed to enjoy showering Tova with extravagant gifts and trips. Heck, there'd been a steady flow of gifts for Kiki too. The way to Tova's heart was through her dog. (I admit, I knew the feeling.) Expensive dog bowls, clothing, collars, barrettes, and just last week a new leather carrier.

"You know those pink booties under the glass counter?"

I looked down. "Sure. I'm looking at them right now."

They were pretty adorable, if I did say so myself. Christmas was three weeks away. The soft pink booties with Swarovski crystals would make the perfect present.

"Wrap me up a pair. I . . ." A loud discussion sparked in the background. "I'm sorry, Mel. Hold on just a second." There was some crackling noise as he covered the phone, but I could still hear pieces of his conversation. "Gwen, Annabelle's chin implant shouldn't take longer than an hour. Tell Mrs. Ides I'll see her at four."

Chin implant? As titillating as that topic was, I tuned it out and surreptitiously watched Wacky Vera pull a package of handwipes from the medical bag she called a purse and proceed to wipe down the chair she'd been sitting on. Once she finished, she tackled the front door with concise vertical strokes, making high-pitched squeaking noises — the glass, that is, not Vera. Disinfectant and bleach hung in the air.

I shook my head and chuckled. I was flanked by crazy people. Heck, maybe I was the crazy one. I tapped my fingers on the counter, waiting for Dr. O to resume our conversation.

"I'm sorry," he apologized suddenly. "Mel, wrap 'em up, and I'll stop by after my last appointment. Remind me, what time do you close?"

"I'm open late for a private party. Ava Rose is launching her new doggie couture line. I'll be here until at least nine."

Vera carefully held her used wipes at arm's length looking for a place to dispose of them. I pointed at the wastebasket next to me, behind the counter.

"Fine. Fine," Dr. O said. "You have my credit card on file. Oh, and a card."

"Pardon?"

"I need a card. And would you write on it? 'I'm sorry we fought.' "

I rolled my eyes. Tova had probably picked the fight just to get make-up presents. "Sure. Did you want me to put Tova's name on the envelope?"

He paused for a couple of seconds. I could hear his name being paged in the background again. "No. Kiki. I gotta go. I'll see you tonight."

I squeezed the phone. Did he just say Kiki? Seriously? He wanted me to address the card to Tova's dog?

What kind of fight could he possibly have had with a five-pound Yorkipoo?

More importantly, who won?

# CHAPTER TWO

Over the years, I've decided there are three kinds of people in Laguna Beach — art lovers, animal lovers, and everyone else. I'm firmly in the animal-lover camp. So were the twenty clients milling around Bow Wow Boutique.

Tonight I was launching a new environmentally friendly dog clothing line by Ava Rose, an up-and-coming designer. I'd invited a handful of my most loyal customers and their guests for a private showing and after-hours Christmas shopping.

Traditional Christmas music energized the room, and hot apple cider warmed the crowd. Twinkling white lights wrapped the trees lining the city streets, reminding us it was the season for giving. Or, for some in town, time to outspend their closest friends.

I'd dressed up for the occasion. Black, leather-kneed leggings, red cashmere tunic, and green plaid flats. To top it all off, I'd traded my daily ponytail for a blow out and soft curls. (Long hair and a ponytail went together like warm peanut butter cookies and milk.) My mama would say tonight's look was a huge improvement over my typical jeans, T-shirt, and motorcycle boots. I might look more presentable, but I wasn't as comfortable.

It was well after eight, and the crowd had thinned. My trusty sidekick, Missy, my English Bulldog, was sound asleep on her dog bed in my office. She wasn't much of a party animal.

Kimber Shores glided to my side, her Pug, Noodles, trailing along behind her. "Mel, I love, love, love this sweater vest. When did you get it?" She brushed my cheek with a perfect air kiss.

Kimber's naturally beautiful and genuinely nice. Always has a kind word to say and has attended every Bow Wow event with credit card in hand. She's one of my most loyal clients. I adore her and Noodles, who always looks a little startled to me.

"Ava Rose brought me a sample a couple of months ago. Isn't it amazing? All her clothing is made from bamboo fiber. I knew it would be perfect for Noodles. Brown and teal are his colors. And who doesn't like argyle?"

"It's so soft." She rubbed the sweater against her cheek. "Thank you for thinking of us." She squeezed my forearm in excitement. "Where is the designer? I just have to meet her."

I pointed her in Ava Rose's direction, relieved someone else would have to listen to her expound on bamboo, the "amazing grass stalk and renewable resource." Don't get me wrong, I'm totally on board with the Go Green train, but I can only spend so long talking about bamboo and how it's used to make everything from houses to socks.

I noticed I was running low on lime-green leads, so I slipped into the back and grabbed a handful. I checked on Missy, who snored noisily, oblivious to the animated chatter out front. I kissed the top of her head then returned to my clients. As I hung the leads on an end cap, I overhead Tova and her assistant, Stacie, talking about the nail polish.

"Puppy Kisses Pink is perfect. It matches Kiki's leash," Tova purred in her sexy model voice. She really is a model. A lingerie model with all the curves that label infers.

My gag reflex reacted instinctively at her saccharine tone.

Kiki was a tiny bundle of excited puppy love on four short legs. I'm not a toy dog kinda gal, but Kiki makes me rethink my stance every time I see her.

"It matches your newest trinket from Dr. O'Doggle," Stacie pointed at Tova's left wrist. I caught a glimpse of the "trinket" — a beautiful pink diamond tennis bracelet that had to be worth a handful of nose jobs.

"Did you see the pink silk dress on the wall? Wouldn't it look adorable on Kiki?" Tova carried her Yorkiepoo over for a closer look. "Wouldn't you love this dress, sweetie pie?"

I went over to Tova. "It's a flower-girl dress. It's handmade, silk and organza. She wouldn't have to wear it to a wedding, but that was the intention behind the design."

Stacie shot a sly smile at Tova, her hazel eyes sharing some radical secret. "It's purrfect."

Stacie was an athletic beauty with thick, honey-blonde locks that brushed her shoulders. Unfortunately, next to Tova's statuesque height and long, auburn hair, Stacie looked short and average. Not a good look for any woman wanting to stand out from the desperate-housewives crowd.

Tova looked momentarily torn, but the look vanished as quickly as the bag of leftover Halloween candy I'd eaten before the first weekend in November. I have a thing for candy corn. The original — yellow, orange, and white. "If you're interested, let me know. I only have the one left in Kiki's size."

As Tova was about to say something, her cell rang. She checked her caller ID. A take-me-now bedroom look swept across her face. "Hi, Jack," she breathed into the phone.

I started to walk away and give her some much needed privacy when her perfectly plucked eyebrows furrowed. I halted in my tracks in a moment of shock. Her eyebrows actually moved. I mean, she is dating a plastic surgeon. He could fix that.

"I see. Are you going to the gym?" she snapped, her tone arctic. I knew that tone well, having used it occasionally on my on-again fiancé, Grey.

"I see," she bit out.

She didn't look happy. Nope. Her eyes hardened, and her collagen lips flattened. Even her curves looked dangerous.

She turned, narrowing her I'll-make-you-pay-for-standing-me-up gaze on me, but spoke into the phone. "Jack darling, I'll be waiting for you. Please don't disappoint me."

Yowser. I recognized that passive-aggressive tone. My mama's famous for perfecting it. Why Tova needed to throw her visual daggers in my direction as she played the guilt card was beyond me, but I'd just as soon she left me out of it. I had my own issues with a no-show man.

As usual, Grey was currently out of town on business. Top secret, undercover, FBI-type business, but more about that later. Back to Tova and her daggers.

She tossed her cell in her handbag and wiggle-walked toward the counter. Her Diane von Furstenberg lace dress was a size too small, which meant it had to be a double zero.

"Melinda, Jack said he had you set aside a gift for Kiki."

"Well, yes. This morning. He said he'd be here this evening to pick it up."

"He's running late and won't be coming. You can just give it to me now."

Okay, this was awkward. I knew the pink boots were for Tova's dog, but Dr. O hadn't told me to hand over the gift to her. What if he wanted it to be a surprise for Kiki? What if he needed it for a get-out-of-Tova-jail free gift? And if he really did want me to hand it over to her now, why didn't he just ask to talk to me?

"It's not that I don't believe you . . ." I cleared my throat. Honestly, I didn't fully believe her. "I'd feel better if I talked to Dr. O personally before I hand you his purchase. It's Bow Wow policy." Okay, not really, but maybe I needed to write up a policy just for these types of situations.

"He's out of surgery and heading for the gym. He wanted me to have it. Now."

"I think he wanted Kiki to have it. Just a small correction." I smiled and reached out to pet the dog.

Tova pulled her away. "You're being difficult. You're always difficult with me. You know he bought Kiki a gift, and you know he was picking it up tonight. We're here now. Just give us the present." Out came the demanding hand and pouty lip I hated so much.

Well, when you ask so sweetly . . . "Give me a minute." I flipped though my business card holder, looking for the doc's information.

It was easy enough to make a quick call to Dr. O's office. If he said it was okay, she could have the boots. Anything to get rid of Miss Bossy Pants and her assistant.

They roamed the shop while I hunted through my stash of business cards. I really needed to get these organized. No. What I needed was to invest in a software system that merged my client database with my cash register, but I was always too busy helping customers. I needed part-time help, but I hadn't had any good candidates. Wacky Vera, a prime example of my options, wasn't going to cut it. I made a mental reminder to look through the applications again tomorrow.

"Tova got stood up again?" Kimber appeared out of nowhere.

"It sounds like there was an emergency, and Dr. O'Doggle won't be able to make it." I wasn't about to insinuate myself into gossip about Tova. I wasn't her biggest fan, but that didn't mean I had to share my unkind thoughts about her with other customers.

Kimber leaned against the counter and spoke quietly. "He stands her up almost every Sunday night. If I were her, I'd hire a P.I. and find out who the other woman is."

"What other woman?" I asked before I could stop myself. So much for staying out of Tova's personal life.

"I've heard he has another girlfriend in Newport. It could even be a wife. Either way, I wouldn't stand for it." Kimber set Noodles' sweater vest next to the cash register.

Another woman? Highly unlikely. If that were true, Tova would have found a way to get rid of the competition. As for a wife, Tova was annoying and superficial, but she didn't seem the kind to steal another woman's husband.

Maybe the sexy Dr. Jack O'Doggle could take only so much Tova and needed a break. Just like the rest of us. After I rang up Kimber's merchandise, I'd call Dr. O and get his okay to cough up Kiki's gift. It was the least I could do.

# CHAPTER THREE

The next day was one of those foggy winter mornings. A spongy wetness hung in the air, a familiar friend to any oceanside town. In a couple of hours, the sun would banish the low-lying clouds and create a golden paradise in its place.

My best bud, Darby Beckett, and I walked our dogs down the Pacific Coast Highway (PCH to us locals), past the sleeping shops, with Koffee Klatch drinks in hand. Darby was in full Annie Hall mode today — wide-legged trousers, white, long-sleeved shirt, and a tweed vest. I sported my usual denim and cotton.

Fluffy, a pretentious but misunderstood Afghan Hound, was now officially Darby's dog. To catch you up to speed on Fluffy, I had inherited the "dog actor" when her owner was murdered. Fluffy and my bull-dog, Missy, weren't a good fit. Missy's a down-home kinda gal. Fluffy is beyond pampered with a capital P. They didn't make good roommates.

But Fluffy and Darby . . . as opposite as they were, needed each other. Once a few legal papers had been filed, Darby and Fluffy were officially a pair. Everyone was happy.

"So tell me about the calendar project. Who's in?" I asked.

Darby owned Paw Prints, a pet photography shop, which was conveniently located next door to Bow Wow. She'd come up with a fantastic idea to shoot a calendar of prominent businesswomen and their pets as a fundraiser for the local Animal Rescue League.

"Well, you and Missy, Shar Summers and Babycakes, Mandy Beenerman and Nietzsche, Cheryl Dolacki and Nemo." She paused to sip her white mocha latte.

Shar was a teenaged TV star, Mandy owned a chain of local exercise studios, and Cheryl drew a cartoon strip that featured her Jack Russell, Nemo. All fitting choices but not nearly enough subjects to complete the calendar.

"I asked Tova and Kiki."

That made sense. Tova was a model. I grunted acceptance. Missy took that as an invitation to sniff the trees in front of the music store. Fluffy waited impatiently, nose in the air.

"I also asked Caro and Dogbert. If I can find a way to work in the cats, I'll include Thelma and Louise too." Darby's tone dared me to disagree.

I stifled a gasp at my cousin's name. "You. Did. Not." Caro and I weren't speaking.

"You had to realize I was going to ask her. She's highly respected."

"She's a pet shrink."

All right, I admit it, "shrink" sounded silly, but in truth, Caro is a damn fine animal behaviorist. A secret sense of pride beats in my heart, knowing how much my beautiful cousin has overcome the last few years. She's worked hard for her success.

"If she weren't your cousin, you wouldn't poke fun. In fact, you'd recommend her."

"If she wasn't a brooch-stealing, get-her-feelings-hurt-by-the-truth kind of cousin." Displeasure and annoyance quashed any positive feeling I'd had for my hardheaded, beautiful cousin.

Darby tossed her empty cup into a public trash can then walked on. "From everything you've told me, the two of you would be on speaking terms if you'd be the bigger person and apologize."

I swallowed the last of my chai latte. I held

my empty cup out, waiting for the next can we passed. "Why do I have to be the one to say I'm sorry? It wasn't my husband who violated the shrink oath and slept with my client. I'm not the one who thought she could save the big idiot from himself and the law. I'm just the loud-mouthed, caring cousin who pointed out the obvious. Caro needs to stop trying to save the world."

Darby slid a wry smile in my direction. "And you wonder why you two aren't talking."

"Nope, I don't wonder. I know exactly why. Caro is sensitive. And she holds a grudge."

Darby shook her head, blonde curls slapping her cheeks. "You spoke out of turn, and you know it, which is why you won't talk to her. You owe her an apology."

I chewed on what she said for a couple of blocks. When we approached a trash can, I tossed my now-mangled cup inside. Obviously, she was right, but for the life of me, I couldn't come up with a believable rebuttal. I could pull out the stock, "You don't know what you're talking about," but after two years, Darby kinda knew my business. That's what best friends do. Keep you honest. Hold you to your word.

Feeling a sudden chill, I pulled my denim

jacket tightly across my chest. "Stop watching those self-help talk shows. You're starting to sound like Caro." It was the best I could come up with. I'd learned during my pageant years: if you can't answer honestly, deflect.

Darby shot me a winning smile. "Thanks." She would take it as a compliment.

I changed the subject back to the calendar. "We have to find a way for you and Fluffy to participate. I could take the picture. You'd have to set the shot up, but I can press the camera button."

"We'll see." Darby was wisely noncommittal.

We walked in silence, traffic occasionally whizzing past, filling in our quiet. The closer we got to the boutique and studio, the harder the dogs strained against their leashes. Everyone was excited to get to work. Except for Missy, who was probably ready for a morning snooze.

It was only nine o'clock, leaving me a couple of hours until I opened for business. I mentally listed all the mini-projects I wanted to complete in the next two hours, starting with finding the last of my Christmas decorations for the boutique. Darby's sudden, excited whisper broke my concentration.

"Oh, my gosh, Mel. Is that Dr. O'Doggle sitting on the bench in front of Bow Wow?"

It sure wasn't Bob, the homeless surfer dude who shows up most mornings. Bob lives out of his Volkswagen van. He has a thing for my dog treats. And before you ask, no, he doesn't have a homeless dog. Bob just likes the treats. I manage to slip him some cash every once in a while just to make sure he's eating real food too.

Dr. O looked like he'd just rolled out of bed. His designer suit was wrinkled, silk tie askew, hair ruffled to the point it looked uncombed, and his Wayfarer Ray-Bans sat cockeyed on his nose. He looked like an upscale bum. His head was tilted sideways, as if he were watching something interesting. One arm was propped on the back of the bench.

Now, I don't pretend to know Dr. O'Doggle all that well, but I have never seen him look unkempt. The man wears custom-tailored operating scrubs, for goodness sakes. He and Tova must have had one heck of a fight. I couldn't come up with one good reason as to why he'd chosen to crash in front of my shop. Unless he needed a very big apology gift.

"Good morning."

He didn't respond. Was he asleep?

Missy sniffed Dr. O's shoes, and Fluffy sniffed his, uh, man parts.

Darby's faced turned fifty shades of embarrassed. She tugged Fluffy back. "Stop, girl. Sorry. Dr. O'Doggle?"

He didn't say a word. He just remained slouched on the bench staring at us. At least, I assumed his eyes were open. With his dark sunglasses, it was hard to know for certain.

"So, are you here about the gift for Kiki?" I asked, relieved I hadn't caved and handed it over to Tova. "Looks like you've had a rough night."

Fluffy whined and stretched her long neck toward Jack. Darby pulled on the leash at the same time Fluffy stepped back and sneezed.

"Bless you," we said.

Dr. O continued to give us the silent treatment. Fluffy eyed him intently. I studied him too.

Darby must have relaxed her grip on the leash. Fluffy took advantage. The big Afghan lunged toward Dr. O'Doggle and knocked him over.

The doctor rolled off the bench and dropped with a thud at our feet.

My stomach knotted. "No, no, no." I shook my head. "Not again."

I shoved Missy's leash in Darby's hand then knelt down and shook his shoulders. "Dr. O'Doggle?" I grabbed his suit lapels and yelled, "Jack?"

Nothing. No, "I'm fine." No, "Stop yelling in my face." No, "Get your hands off me."

No, no, no.

I checked his throat for a pulse. Nothing. But he was still warm. My fingers brushed against something that felt familiar, and I'm not talking about his tie. I pulled back his shirt for a better look. I sucked in a breath, my nose filled with a light female perfume I didn't recognize. A thin dog leash was wound tightly around his neck.

This was not an accident.

"Is he . . . ?" Darby asked softly.

I looked up at her. "Dead. No more late night walks for him."

# CHAPTER FOUR

Darby shivered. "Maybe he had a heart attack."

I sighed and sat down by the body. The coldness from the cement quickly seeped through my jeans. I barely noticed. "That'd be nice." But doubtful.

Missy yawned. She sat and stared at the front door of the boutique. Fluffy looked at Darby, nose in the air, as if she was above such distasteful situations.

"There's something around his neck," I said quietly.

Darby patted her head absently. "You mean his tie?"

I shook my head no. "A dog leash." I immediately recalled how angry Tova had been last night that Dr. O wasn't coming. Had she been angry enough to kill him? Tova was demanding and annoying, but a killer? I didn't think so. "We need to call 9-1-1."

Darby did a double take, her blue eyes

huge. "Detective Malone isn't going to be happy to see us."

Darby was right. Calling the police meant homicide detective Judd Malone would show up. He wouldn't be thrilled I'd tripped over another dead body. (For those of you counting, this is body number three.)

"I don't understand. Dr. O was fine last night. Why did he have to die here?" I looked at Darby knowing my eyes reflected the anxiety bubbling inside. "You should call Malone. Give him a heads up. I'll call 9-1-1."

Darby shook her head. "No way." She pointed at the dead man. "He was here to see you. You call the police."

I stood and brushed sand and dirt from my backside. "Just because this is his, ah, almost final resting place, doesn't mean he was here to see me. Come on Darb, Malone likes you better."

"That's not saying much."

Warming to the idea, I smiled reassuringly and held out my fist. "Rock, paper, scissors? Loser calls Malone."

"Mel, he's used to getting these types of calls from you."

Ouch. "Which is why you should call him."

My buddy studied me for a nanosecond

before holding her fist in front of her. God love Darby Beckett. She was my best friend for a reason.

"One, two, three," we counted in unison.

I held out my fist.

Rock.

Darby held out her hand, palm down.

Paper.

Paper covers rock.

I looked up at her with my practiced beauty queen smile, holding my breath. "Best two out of three?"

Not everyone has a homicide detective on speed dial. I do. I'd prefer not to analyze that peculiarity. Especially since Judd Malone didn't have a lot of patience for me. After losing that silly childhood game with Darby (I should have offered to flip a quarter, at least then I'd have had a fifty-fifty chance), I called Detective Malone to explain the situation. He told me to touch nothing and to keep everyone away. Yeah, I unfortunately already knew the routine.

Darby and I tried to act nonchalant. Most downtown businesses didn't open until ten or eleven. It wasn't tourist season, so it was fairly quiet on the streets. The way I figured, we'd upheld our end of the deal.

It was the police, blaring down the street,

who drew attention, red and blue lights flashing in the low clouds. The few shop owners who were already at work spilled out into the sidewalk, circling my shop. Asking questions I didn't want to answer.

You know the saying, "There's no such thing as bad press?" It's not true. A dead body lying in front of your business is bad press. There's just no getting around it. Especially when the body in question was a new customer.

Bless her heart, Darby had wrangled the dogs inside Paw Prints. That left me to hover over Dr. O's corpse and shoo away the rubberneckers.

"What happened?"

That was Detective Malone. A man of few words. Occasionally, I wondered if he was a man of fewer friends. He was extremely good looking in that heart-stopping way, but he had the personality of a souvenir paperweight.

I faced Malone, happy to concentrate on someone alive. He'd arrived in his detective uniform — jeans, T-shirt, and leather jacket. It was very similar to my usual dress, the main difference being I wore mostly dog-inspired graphic tees. Today my T-shirt read, "You had me at woof."

My eyes narrowed on Malone. "As I said

on the phone, Darby and I found him like this. Well, sort of. He was sitting on the bench, looking like a bum, but then Fluffy, you remember Fluffy, well she took it upon herself to sniff, uh . . . him, and then he tumbled off the bench and whacked his head on the cement."

"Did you touch him?" Malone gave me his signature stone-faced cop look. Having recently been on the receiving end of that look more times than one could count, I was immune.

"I checked for a pulse. But that's it. As you're aware, I'm not a fan of dead people." I glanced over my shoulder at Dr. O'Doggle, his crumpled body still in a heap in front of the bench.

"Yet somehow you continue to find them."

"Yeah, well, there are just some things a girl can't control. Apparently, for me, it's dead bodies. I have to be good at something."

"Detective Malone," a female crime scene tech called out.

"Don't leave," Malone ordered.

I rolled my eyes. "Where would I go?"

The tech gently rolled Doc over then pointed toward his back. Malone blinked, leaning in for a closer look. I wanted to see, too. Was it the green leash they were looking at? They didn't need to move him to see that.

I stood on my tiptoes and swayed side-to-side, angling for a better view. I didn't see anything odd or unusual, but something had piqued the police's interest, which in turn piqued my curiosity.

Malone mumbled something under his breath only the tech could hear. She nodded. A couple of uniformed officers asked me to step back as they taped off the area around Dr. O, which happened to include the front door to Bow Wow.

"Uh, you can't do that. My customers won't be able to get into my store." Once word got out about Jack, I'd have plenty of foot traffic. Not a whole lot of purchasing, but a ton of gossiping. That's just how it worked here.

"Mel, you know the drill. This is a potential crime scene," Officer Salinas ground out.

"Thanks for the reminder." This wasn't my first two-step with Salinas. He hadn't been receptive to my Texas charms the last time I'd wanted to enter a crime scene, either. All I'd wanted then was to go inside Fluffy's owner's home and retrieve Fluffy's hairbrush and a towel. You'd think I'd threatened to take Salinas' cop car on a joy ride through our little oceanside town.

I have to commend myself, though. I was handling this situation much better than the last one. I only felt like throwing up. The lack of blood on Doc's body made a huge difference.

I checked my watch, just after ten. Customers would start trickling in soon. I didn't want to sound insensitive, but I needed to know if a schedule shuffle was in order.

"Salinas, how long do you think you'll be?"

"Longer if you keep talking to me." He continued to stretch bright yellow police tape across Bow Wow's front door. Dang, this was bad for business. Bad, bad, bad.

Darby popped out of her studio and made her way toward me. She'd found a black-felt pea coat to ward off the chill. I noticed she avoided Malone. "What'd I miss?" she asked.

"Nothing. Malone doesn't want us to leave. He has questions."

"I don't like his questions." Darby had every reason to be wary. It wasn't that long ago when she and Malone were at odds. He thought she'd killed Mona Michael, Fluffy's original owner. You couldn't blame him. The evidence at the time pointed in Darby's direction. It certainly didn't help that she'd kept a major secret from all of us.

Malone noticed Darby standing next to me. He finished his conversation and then made his way back to where we waited.

"Ms. Beckett." His mouth split into what I'm sure he thought was a smile. Man, it needed a lot of work.

"Detective Malone." Her voice cracked. Nerves.

I winked at her in an effort to boost her confidence. Darby wrung her hands then caught herself and tucked them in her jean pockets.

"When the two of you arrived, was anyone hanging around?" he asked.

"Not really," I said.

Darby cleared her throat. "Mr. Forester across the street arrived at his shop about the same time we did. But that's all. This place doesn't usually get busy until eleven."

"No customers, delivery trucks, pedestrians?"

I shrugged. "I wasn't really paying attention. I was thinking about what I had to do today."

"He was here to see you specifically?" he asked.

I wanted to look offended, but I couldn't pull it off. "I suppose. I overheard an argument between him and Tova last night when he called her. He planned to pick up a gift for Kiki during the private party I threw last night for a new designer. But something came up, and he never showed."

"Did he say why he wasn't coming?"

I shook my head. "I never talked to him. Just Tova."

He narrowed his eyes and asked, "Are you sure she was talking to him on the phone, not to someone else?"

"Well, not one hundred percent. But I did see her caller ID, and it said Jack, so I assumed that's who she was talking to."

"Did she mention how he sounded?"

"Tova usually only talks about herself," I explained.

He nodded and scribbled mysterious notes in his black notebook. "When did you speak to the doctor last?"

"Yesterday morning." When I didn't elaborate, he motioned with his hand for me to continue. I sighed. "It was nothing. He called in between surgeries and asked me to set aside a pair of dog booties for Kiki. Tova's dog."

"Is that the gift you mentioned earlier?"

I nodded.

"And neither of you know why he didn't show up last night?"

"I wasn't at the party," Darby offered.

"Ms. Langston didn't invite you?" he asked evenly.

Darby threw her shoulders back and mustered her moxie. "I had plans."

"How's Fluffy?"

Darby blinked rapidly, completely caught off guard. "Fine. We're fine. Thank you for asking."

He nodded. "Ms. Langston, how was Dr. O'Doggle acting the last time you talked to him?"

I frowned, not sure what he was getting at. "What do you mean?"

"Happy, sad, scared, depressed?" he rattled off the emotions as if he were reciting his grocery list.

I shook my head. "I don't know. We talked over the phone. I don't know him all that well."

"What about Tova?" Mr. Personality asked.

"She was ticked off. And impatient." Boy, was I familiar with the latter.

"Do you know how he died?" Darby asked the one question on both our minds.

He slapped his notebook closed and tucked it into his inner jacket pocket. He gave us the don't-ask-questions look. "Too early to know for sure."

What he was really saying was it's none of

our business. But it was, as long as Dr. O'Doggle lay dead in front of Bow Wow.

"I know you and your crew have a lot to do. Should I take the day off, or will I be able to open for business today?" I motioned to the activity behind us.

"I'm sure you can find something to do for a couple of hours."

Well, there was something I needed to do. An important something I'd put off for too long. "Do I need to call before I come back?" I asked.

"You'll know when we're finished."

Wow. Such a communicator.

# CHAPTER FIVE

I don't mean to sound uncaring, but finding murder victims has become, well I don't want to say routine, but it's not as unusual as it should be for someone who's not a cop. Missy and I left Darby and Fluffy at Paw Prints and headed to Glitter, the local jewelry shop. A couple weeks ago I'd once again recovered my brooch from my cousin, Caro. A family heirloom, the pin was a multi-jeweled basket of fruit as ugly as a Texas armadillo and equally tough.

It belonged to our Grandma Tillie, who'd left it to "her favorite granddaughter." That was me. Of course, Caro thought it was her. For either of us to just hand it over to the other would be unthinkable. We're Montgomery women. Montgomery women do not roll over and accept defeat. We Texans handle our differences our own way.

Caro had been at her trickiest and had used herself as a decoy (she's a smart lady), convincing her new friend and neighbor, April Mae June, to steal my brooch right out from under my nose. I was more than a little miffed at her ingenious heist.

I'd plotted, planned, and schemed before finding my pin in Caro's dresser drawer. I'd been so excited, I'd worn it to Mewsings, a local art show. Mewsings exhibited artwork painted by felines, not humans. Surprisingly, the show had been a huge success. I still didn't get what all the buzz was about.

The look on Caro's face had been priceless when she'd realized I'd stolen the brooch back. Of course, the shocked look on my face was equally priceless when I realized she also wore Grandma Tillie's pin. My cunning cousin had had a duplicate made.

I needed to know if I had the real one, so I'd dropped my copy off at Glitter for an appraisal. Grant Trask, the owner, had called a few days ago to let me know I did, indeed, have the original.

Now it was time to pick it up and take it home, where it was safe from my sneaky cousin.

"Hey, Gloria. How's business?"

She came from behind the counter and greeted me with a handshake, Missy with a loving head rub. Gloria's apple cheeks were full of warmth. "Good, good. How about you?" her voice quavered.

I thought about the murder scene in front of Bow Wow. "My life is always interesting. I'm here to pick up the brooch. Is it ready?"

Gloria didn't move. Not even a blink. I immediately had a bad feeling. "The brooch?" she squeaked.

"I brought it in a couple of weeks ago."

She ran her hands down the sides of her sweater, smoothing invisible wrinkles. "Yes. Right after the cat art show at the Arman Gallery."

I nodded. "I waited to pick it up until I had a hiding place. You know Caro, she can't be trusted."

Gloria nodded slowly as she inched her way back behind the counter. "That Caro. She's a wily one. I thought Grant had called you."

My breath caught. "You don't have it, do you?"

Gloria clasped her hands together. "No. I'm sorry Mel. I'm so sorry. Caro came and picked it up yesterday."

"But I dropped it off. Why would ya'll hand it over to her?" I'd worked extremely hard to lose my Texas twang. But it was times like this when it would not be denied.

For those of you who know the story, I'd

pulled a similar shifty tactic on Caro earlier this year. As much as I want to say that I was justified, we all know the only difference is that I came out the winner.

I hated losing.

If Grandma Tillie were alive, she'd look me in the eye and tell me not to get all "het up" about it. But she wasn't alive. And I was more than "het up." I was fixin' to track down my cousin and yank my brooch out of her iron fist.

"I'm sorry," Gloria whispered. "Zane didn't realize."

Zane, the owner's nephew, was the same young man I had sweet-talked into giving me the brooch.

Hells bells. Karma stinks.

# CHAPTER SIX

Malone and his crew were still gathering evidence when Missy and I returned to Bow Wow. Salinas noticed us right away and explained they needed an additional thirty minutes. I wondered if the police were questioning Tova. She didn't seem the type to hold up well under police scrutiny.

Wanting to lick my wounds without an audience, Missy and I meandered into Paw Prints. Darby was setting up for a photo shoot when we arrived.

I unleashed Missy, who trotted over to the sheepskin rug and joined Fluffy. They greeted each other as all dogs do. I was grateful to be a human, able to just fist-bump anyone I hadn't seen in an hour.

"We're back. Are you free to grab some lunch?" I called out.

"Sure, let me finish up here. What do you have in mind?"

"No rush. How about a portabella burger?" I dropped with dramatic flair onto the Victorian couch and watched Darby move a wooden bench, searching for the perfect angle.

"When do you shoot Caro?" I'd like to shoot my cousin about now.

"Next week. Why?" Darby asked.

"She's got the brooch."

Darby stopped fiddling with the fall backdrop and turned in my direction. "But how? It was at the jewelry shop. You just got it back."

"Nope." I propped my feet up on the scuffed coffee table and stared at my boots. "She beat me there. Grant's nephew returned it to the wrong cousin. Caro stole it right out from under my nose. Again."

Only difference? This time Caro hadn't used her new sticky-finger friend with three names. I wasn't sure about that little Tinkerbell girl, April Mae June. She appeared sweet and vulnerable, but that gal was sneaky and a thief. Just like Caro.

"Do you have a plan?" Darby asked.

"Not yet. While she's with you, I think I'll let myself into her place and search for it."

Darby bit her lip, holding back what I knew was a smile. "I'm sure you'll come up with something. You always do."

I stood, brushed off my jeans and took a

deep breath. "Oh, please. You're thinking what I've already said aloud. Payback stinks. Caro's a worthy adversary, but in the end, I'm going to win. That's my brooch." I pointed to the autumn set-up she was fussing over. "Who's coming? Anyone I know?"

"Cheryl and Nemo. I think they'll make a lovely October, don't you?" Darby raked some scattered silk leaves into a pile.

"Do you want help?" I asked.

Darby held out the plastic rake.

We worked quickly. Darby had a great eye for creating a realistic nature setting. I couldn't wait to see what she came up with for Missy and me.

Cheryl and her pooch arrived right on time. Nemo strained to greet his cohorts, but Cheryl wasn't ready to let him off his lead. She was a tall lady with warm eyes. She penned a successful cartoon strip starring Nemo. Think Marmaduke but with a super-smart Jack Russell Terrier.

For the past month, the comic strip story involved Nemo escaping from the backyard and all the elaborate contraptions his owners built to outsmart the little guy. Yet he'd always found a way out. Knowing the athleticism of the breed, I believed the comic was heavily biographical.

Darby greeted her clients and made quick

introductions.

"I love your comic," I gushed. "I read it to Missy all the time."

"Thank you." She smiled shyly, pushing a lock of light brown curls off her face. "You own the dog boutique next door right?"

"That's right."

She shifted her weight. "Did you know the police are in front of your shop?"

Darby and I exchanged a look. Thank goodness the coroner had already removed the body.

Word was bound to get out eventually. Time for damage control.

"Do you know Dr. Jack O'Doggle, the plastic surgeon in Newport?" I asked.

Nemo paced alongside Cheryl. She pointed her index finger at the floor and told him to sit. He quickly obeyed, tail wagging, waiting for her next command. Instead, she returned her attention to us. "I've heard of him."

"Darby and I found him dead in front of Bow Wow this morning."

She gasped. "Are you both okay? What happened?"

"A little shaken up, but fine," Darby reassured her.

Missy waddled over to see what was going on. She snorted and sniffed Nemo and

51

found him acceptable. Nemo tipped his brown eyes toward his owner, begging for his freedom.

"You can let him off his lead anytime you want," Darby said. "Don't worry about Fluffy. She keeps to herself, and Missy's already accepted him into the pack."

Cheryl gave Nemo a couple of instructions before turning him loose. Once he was off the leash, he raced around the room excitedly, with Missy bringing up the rear.

"What happened to the doctor?" Cheryl asked.

"We're not sure," I said.

"Do the police think he died of natural causes?"

Darby and I looked at each other again. I shrugged, uncertain of how much to say. "Detective Malone likes to keep his information to himself."

The dogs dropped a ball at Cheryl's feet. She tossed it across the room. They tore off after it. "I have a friend in the plastic surgery business. She said there have been some shady dealings in his office."

"Like what?" I asked.

"Accusations that he was poaching patients from other surgeons, lawsuits. I wonder if the stress got to him, and he had a heart attack."

I didn't think so. I think someone strangled him with a dog lead. That reminded me. I wanted to research something on my office computer.

I called Missy and excused myself from the photo shoot. We headed for the boutique. Salinas and his crew were gone, but Malone was loitering in front of Bow Wow. Now what?

# CHAPTER SEVEN

I led Malone inside. Missy charged for her water bowl and splashed water everywhere under the pretense of drinking. Malone cased the place without turning his head.

"I see you got the call you could open the shop."

"No. I was next door with Darby. Just luck that I was leaving at the same time ya'll finished. Did you suddenly get a dog, or are you here to ask me more questions?"

He pulled out a beautiful, pink-diamond tennis bracelet from his pocket. "Do you recognize this?"

Of course I did. I swallowed past the lump in my throat. "How'd you get it?"

"Do you know who it belongs to?"

I'd read enough mystery books to know he already knew, no sense in evading his question. "Tova Randall."

"How do you know it belongs to Tova?"

"She wore it last night at the party."

He dropped the jewelry into a small baggie then returned it to his pocket. "Thanks."

"Any news on how he died?"

He picked up a pink birthday hat. "Nothing solid."

"When I felt for a pulse, I noticed he was wearing a dog leash."

He didn't blink, just stood there. Like a very irritated cop. The party hat in his hand only made him look more dangerous.

"And," he prompted.

I walked over to the green leads I'd restocked last night. "I'm almost positive it was this one." I traded the lead for the hat.

"Do you track who you've sold these to?"

"Sort of. I can tell how many I've sold, when and if they paid by credit card, cash, or check. If they paid by credit card or check, I can find out who purchased one."

"Do you remember who you sold one to recently?"

"I sold one to Jack O'Doggle last week."

"Anyone else?"

"I can print a list." I headed for the office.

"Hold on. I have an appointment. Pull your records. Do not do anything other than bring them to me. In person. Not by email. Got it?"

"Sure."

We both knew I'd study the list before I

handed it over. I couldn't help it. I was naturally curious. Malone considered me unnaturally nosey. The problem was, he needed me.

It was a heady feeling, knowing I had something he wanted. I liked it.

After a busy day of dodging questions and hand-selling Ava's new line of doggie clothing, Missy and I happily settled into a quiet night at home. Missy snored in her bed while I sipped my favorite cabernet curled up on the couch.

I checked my cell for the hundredth time, making sure I hadn't missed Grey's call. To the outside world, Grey was out of town on a business trip for his art gallery, ACT (which stood for Art Crime Team). In reality, he was in Chicago working on an art fraud case for the FBI.

Obviously, he couldn't share details, but it came down to this: someone lied about something they stole to cheat another party out of their property. That's white-collar crime according to the FBI. (Seriously, it's on their website.)

I set my wine on the end table next to my cell. I'd almost forgotten the list of customer names I'd brought home — people who'd bought one of the deadly green leashes recently.

I quickly retrieved it from my bag then returned to the seat, pulled the blanket off the back of couch, and tossed it over my legs.

I studied the names on the depressingly long list. Fifteen identifiable customers out of twenty-five sales. The rest had paid cash. Right there in black and white was Jack O'Doggle, the only name I recognized. Malone had his work cut out for him. Was someone on this list a killer?

My cell rang. My heart skipped a beat when I saw it was Grey. "Hey." I tried to sound like I wasn't sitting by the phone waiting for his call. Which I wasn't. Really.

"Hi. Are you home?" he asked.

"You bet. Curled up on the couch. How about you? Back at the hotel?"

"Not yet. Soon. Things didn't go as planned. I may not be home for few more days."

He sounded tired. If I could see his face, I could read what he wasn't saying. "But you're safe?"

"I'm fine." After a brief pause he asked, "What's going on?"

Here's the deal — with Grey, it was best to just spit out the facts. In his line of work, word got around fast when his fiancée found another dead body.

"First, I'm fine. Honestly. Darby, I, and the dogs, we're all fine."

"Mel, stop stalling. What's going on?"

"Well, Darby and I found Dr. O'Doggle dead in front of Bow Wow. We called Detective Malone, and he's on the case."

A heavy sigh rushed into my ear. It was the sigh that went hand in hand with him rubbing his head in frustration. "What do you mean by 'found?' "

I gave him the low down, and he grunted his disbelief. "I'm glad you're okay. Be careful. A customer was possibly murdered in front of your shop. Keep your eyes open and stay aware of your surroundings. What did Malone have to say?"

"You know Malone. He keeps everything to himself. Speaking of keeping things to themselves. Caro stole my brooch from Glitter."

Grey sighed again. Only this time with exasperation. "Mel."

"I know. It's payback from when I got to Glitter first and convinced Zane I'd return it to Caro, but you'd think they'd have learned their lesson and made sure they returned the pin to the person who brought it into the store."

"Technically, Caro brought it into the store first."

"That was then. To have it cleaned. I'm talking about now. When I dropped it off for an appraisal. Big difference."

"Have you talked to Caro yet?"

"You know we're not talking. What you really want to know is if I've come up with a plan to get it back."

"No. That's not what I was asking. Look, I have to go. I have a meeting, and I can't be late. Promise me, if you see anything out of the norm, you'll call the police. I should be home by Sunday at the latest."

"I promise. Keep safe. I love you." I worked hard to keep the concern out of my voice. I hated this part of his job.

"Be good and don't pick fights. Love you, too," he said before disconnecting.

Notice I didn't promise anything about not fighting.

# CHAPTER EIGHT

I hadn't slept well. I'd dreamt that a UPS truck dropped off a shipment of green leashes, and I had to sort them in alphabetical order by buyer, which then somehow morphed into Grey, gun drawn, chasing a crazed painter who wore a white beret and a handlebar mustache (very creepy) down the back alleys of Chicago.

After a quick bowl of Cap'n Crunch, I slipped on my favorite True Religion jeans, a pet-themed T-shirt (today's read, "It's all fun and games until someone's wearing a cone"), and boots. I walked Missy around the block so she could do her business.

I decided to leave her home today. The shop was bound to be crazy. Dr. O'Doggle's death was all over the news, including the part about the dog leash and dropping dead at Bow Wow's doorstep. You gotta love the media.

Once Missy was settled, I grabbed my

jacket and headed to the police station to give Malone the list of names. I parked in front of the building and walked inside. The uniformed clerk at the front desk looked up. I recognized her from the last time I had been there, the day Malone had brought Darby in for questioning.

The clerk was a tiny wisp of a woman — all blonde hair, uniform, and gun. I sold dog bowls heavier than her. Since she was armed, I kept most of my smart-alecky comments to myself.

"What can I do for you?" She sized me up.

Did I mention she was all business?

I flashed my trustworthy smile. "Detective Malone asked me to drop off some information."

She cocked a blonde eyebrow at me. "What kind?"

"A list of names. It's in regards to Dr. O'Doggle's death."

"Hold on." She picked up the phone. "Melinda Langston is here with information about the O'Doggle case." She eyed me. "Will do."

"He'll be right here. How's your cousin?"

Well, hell. She remembered me. And Caro. "Peachy. Just peachy."

Malone appeared in his T-shirt and jeans.

"You're out early."

"Good morning to you too, sunshine. I brought you the list." I waved the paper in the air. "I have good news and not so good news."

He snatched it from my outstretched hand. "I'd prefer you didn't have any news."

Undeterred, I continued, following him to his office. "The good news is that Darby's name is nowhere on that list. Just in case you're still suspicious of her since the last murder."

"That is good news."

"The bad news is I sold twenty-five green leads in the last six months, and only half paid with a check or credit card."

We stopped in front of his office. "Do you have addresses?"

"Of course."

Here's the thing about Malone's office. It's barely big enough for Thumbelina, not a man over six feet. He sat behind his desk, and I took the tan plastic chair opposite him. It was my only option.

"Is that stain new?" I pointed at the large brown spot under the garbage can.

He didn't look amused or interested in discussing the cleanliness of his office. Apparently, he was all business today, too.

"My inventory system is down. I was lucky

to get this much. I can put together a list of phone numbers and addresses and drop it off later today. Would that work?" I asked.

"You're not getting any wild ideas are you, Ms. Langston?"

"Don't you think it's time you started calling me Mel? Even Melinda's better than Ms. Langston."

"You didn't answer my question."

He was warming up to me. "Ideas about what? Calling me by my first name?"

"Helping me."

I gave him a wide grin. "I just helped you."

"You know what I mean. Don't poke your nose in police business. If you think of something that might be important, call me. Failing to cooperate with an investigation is a crime. Don't try and sleuth it out yourself."

I held out my hands, palms up. "I wouldn't dream of it."

"It's not your dreams I'm concerned with. You got lucky last time. You could have been killed."

Blah, blah, blah. I was well acquainted with the current song and dance. "I don't have a dog in this fight. I only got involved last time because you refused to believe Darby was innocent."

Malone leaned back in his chair, daring

me to argue. "I go where the evidence takes me."

I got the feeling that might lead toward Tova. I stood. "Sometimes the evidence points to an innocent person."

From the moment I flipped the open sign at Bow Wow, there was a steady stream of customers. Most of them were in the market for gossip and not pet accessories. Except when it came to the green leather leads. Suddenly, everyone wanted one. I loved my customers, but sometimes they were a little over the top, even for me.

In the midst of all the craziness, I'd forgotten about my last phone call with Dr. O. The second Tova's assistant, Stacie, rushed into the shop, I remembered. Kiki's boots were stashed under the counter. Oh, boy. I needed to deliver those to Tova. Not that Tova would be in the mood for the delivery. I regretted not giving her the gift last night.

"Mel, tell me this is just a bad dream," she begged, her eyes red-rimmed.

I was pretty sure she hadn't been crying over her poor choice in fashion. Someone needed to do the girl a favor and tell her skinny jeans and a body-hugging tunic weren't a good wardrobe choice for someone with the muscle definition of a Ukrainian bodybuilder.

As much as I'd love to tell her what she wanted to hear, the crime scene tape stuffed in the public trash can in front of my store would suggest otherwise. Plus, Dr. O's death had made national headlines before noon.

I guided her away from the small group of customers so we could have a semblance of privacy.

"The reporter on TV said Jack's death was undetermined. Have you heard anything?" she asked.

I shook my head. "How's Tova?" I asked.

"I just came from her place. She's distraught. I don't know what to do."

I remembered everything Darby had gone through not that long ago. It had been tough. A couple of times I'd been worried about leaving her alone. Not that I thought she'd harm herself, but because she was terrified of going to jail. It was rough. "Just be there for her. She'll let you know what she needs."

She leaned closer, her brows furrowed. "I think Tova's in a lot of trouble, Mel. I don't know if you've heard, but that detective questioned her."

"I didn't know." But I wasn't surprised.

"He questioned both of us. I happened to

be at her place when he arrived. Tova's convinced the cops believe she was involved with Jack's death. Why else would they come to her house?"

"That's normal. Those closest to the vict . . . deceased are the first people the police talk to. It doesn't always mean anything other than the police are doing their job. What kind of questions did they ask?"

She rubbed the back of her hand. "How well Tova and Jack got along? Have they been fighting? When was the last time I saw Jack? Where was I last night?"

I twitched with curiosity. I wanted to know too. "They seemed like a normal dating couple."

"They were more than dating. They were talking about marriage."

My jaw hit the floor. "Are you kidding me? I didn't realize they were serious."

"If it wasn't for Kiki, Jack would have already proposed. He doesn't like dogs."

What kind of person hates dogs? My opinion of Dr. O'Doggle plummeted. Although, I was suddenly confused. "Then why was he always buying Kiki gifts?"

She rubbed the top of her hand again, nervously. "Tova told him she and Kiki were a package deal. He tried to be nice with Kiki, but she sensed it was all an act. Kiki bit him last week. Jack and Tova had a huge fight, and she kicked him out. He was trying to get back into Tova's good graces."

By kissing up to Kiki? That explained the booties.

Kiki was one of the most well-behaved dogs I knew. At least, I'd thought she was. What had Jack O'Doggle done to her to make her lash out? Or had he done something to Tova? Either way, once Malone learned all this, it wouldn't be good for Team Tova.

"What do you think?" I asked.

"About Jack?" She practically spit out his name.

I nodded.

Her hazel eyes narrowed. "He saw Tova as someone to trot around like arm candy while he broke her heart. He didn't love her the way she deserved."

I stepped back. I wasn't expecting such animosity. If what Stacie believed was true, Tova could be in trouble.

"Does she have a lawyer?" I asked softly.

Stacie blinked rapidly. "Not a criminal lawyer." She started to reach out to me and then thought better. "Why? Do you think she needs one? That's going to fall to me isn't it? I'm her assistant. Somehow, that's going to be my job." She looked ready to burst at the seams with anxiety.

I patted her hand awkwardly. I pulled back slowly, surprised at how rough her skin felt. No wonder she'd been rubbing it.

She covered the back of her hand. "I'm getting over a case of poison ivy."

Great. I needed to wash my hands. Where was that bottle of antibacterial hand cleanser I'd just bought?

"I'm not contagious," she reassured me.

Right. "Look, I'm sure everything will work out."

Notice I didn't assure her it would be okay. In my experience, this type of situation always got worse before it ever got better. I had a strong feeling this time wouldn't be an exception. Dr. O was dead, and if the red marks on his neck could talk, I'm sure they'd scream, "Stop. You're killing me."

The more I thought about it, the more I was convinced, Jack O'Doggle was murdered.

I was also convinced, in spite of what she said, I needed to wash my hands.

# CHAPTER NINE

A little after one, Darby and Fluffy stopped by as I finished ringing up the last customer, a tall blonde with a wide smile. Snob dog, Fluffy, refused to greet me, walking directly toward my office in search of Missy's bed. Darby, dressed in an adorable Jersey knit dress and flats, waited by the dog carriers until I finished.

"I hope Callie enjoys her Christmas sweater." I handed a blue Bow Wow bag to the blonde. Callie was her beautiful Weimaraner. Weimies are a loyal and loving breed. Watching the two browse through the store, it was easy to tell they were soul mates.

"It's perfect for the east coast," she said happily.

"Too bad you had to fly all the way out to southern California to find it," I teased.

She held up the bag. "I'll send you a picture of her wearing it. Merry Christmas."

"Merry Christmas," I called out as she left.

Darby made her way to the counter. "She seemed nice."

I nodded. "She's visiting family for the holidays. Doesn't go anywhere without her four-legged kid."

Darby tucked blonde curls behind her ear. "Speaking of visiting relatives for Christmas, didn't you promise Mitch you'd go home for the holidays?"

Mitch was my brother. Home was Dallas. Mitch recently got married. He and his new bride, Nikki, promised my parents they'd come home for Christmas. He badgered me to agree to the same.

"I didn't specify what Christmas," I hedged.

"Mel," she scolded.

"Don't even bother to try and make me feel guilty. I'm immune."

I lied. A tiny twinge of shame pinched an itty-bitty corner of my heart. My parents still lived in the house we'd grown up in. Sometimes I missed it and the wide-open spaces. And then I remembered Mama and Daddy still lived there — together.

Daddy loved Mama more than a person probably should. She was bossy, manipulative, and demanding. But Daddy, well, he was convinced she had a heart somewhere underneath all that scheming and plotting. As for me, I knew better. But that didn't mean I didn't love her. She was my mama.

I changed the subject. "Stacie dropped by this morning. Malone's already made his rounds to Tova's place."

Darby frowned. "I know what that's like."

I pulled out a couple of stools from behind the counter and patted the one next to me. "According to Stacie, Tova's pretty upset."

"I'm sure she is."

"It sounds like Malone was pretty hard on her. You know how it goes. Friends, lovers, and acquaintances are the first to be questioned."

"And family," she muttered.

"Darby, I don't have a good feeling about this."

"You don't know anything sinister happened."

I gave her a look. "You saw Malone. He's a homicide detective. He didn't hang out here asking about the leashes just to annoy me. No, there's more to this. I think someone strangled Dr. O then dumped him on the bench outside my shop. I thought everyone liked Dr. O. It seems that's not the case. By the way, Stacie said Jack didn't like dogs."

Darby wrinkled her nose. "As horrendous as that sounds, that doesn't lead to murder."

"Why would he have a dog leash wrapped around his neck?"

She blushed. "Maybe he and Tova are into that type of stuff."

I looked at Darby surprised. What had Darby been watching? Or reading? "That's possible. There's one way to find out."

"Mel. You have that tone in your voice. The one that sounds like you're going to do something you shouldn't."

"I'm not going to do anything. I'm just telling you I have a bad feeling. Dr. O'Doggle was a healthy guy. I've seen him run marathons. He works out at the gym daily. He has his scrubs tailored for goodness sakes."

"So someone killed him for his scrubs?" Darby rolled her eyes. "Just because people look healthy doesn't mean they are. Back in Nebraska, when I was a junior in high school, Ben Wright was a running back for our football team. One day during practice, he just died. He had a heart problem no one knew about."

"I stand by my statement that by the look on Malone's face, there's something he's not sharing."

"He doesn't have to share. He's a cop."

"But I have a vested interest. Jack was found dead in front of my store."

"That doesn't mean you're automatically involved."

"No. But Malone's already asked for my help," I said, triumph ringing in my voice.

"He wanted information. Not your help."

"I have all kinds of information: Jack O'Doggle wasn't as loved as I thought. He was in trouble over unethical business practices. You know what else I know? It's possible he was about to pop the question to Tova. But he hated her dog."

"Is she strong enough to strangle him with a dog lead?" Darby mused.

"I think the real question is, how'd she get him to wear the leash in the first place?"

# CHAPTER TEN

My next interview for the part-time position was in less than thirty minutes. Darby and Fluffy went back to the studio while I hoped and prayed Betty Foxx was the assistant of my dreams.

I set out her application and the bottle of antibacterial hand sanitizer on the counter. I arranged a couple of chairs in the back of the shop by the coffee bar. As I straightened stools behind the counter, the door opened.

"Is anyone here?" An older female voice rang out.

I turned toward the door. "Hello, can I help . . ."

Holy Moly.

I didn't mean to be unkind, but my first thought was please, please, please don't be Betty.

"Hi, there. Are you Melody? I'm Betty Foxx."

Of course she was. She stood barely five

feet in her white sneakers and silk, animal-print pajamas. She radiated attitude with her Dreamsicle lipstick eyebrows. Oh, yeah. I was longing for Vera White right now.

"Let's get this over with," I muttered under my breath. "I'm Melinda. Melinda Langston. Have a seat. Did you bring a résumé?"

She followed me toward the two chairs I'd set up earlier. "What's a résumé going to tell you that isn't already on my application? Either you want me or you don't. Don't let my age fool you. I come with experience."

As Grandma Tillie would say, she was a straight shooter. Being a straight shooter myself, I appreciated that about her.

I waited for her to get comfortable. She folded her hands on top of the black patent-leather purse on her lap. "Do I have the job?" An infectious eagerness lit up her face.

I glanced down at her application and held back a chuckle. "I have a couple of questions first. I see you've worked retail."

"I sold cosmetics for years. Before you were born."

My gaze returned to her perfectly applied eyebrows. Grandma Tillie drew on her eyebrows too. That was normal for their generation. Of course, Grandma Tillie used brown eyebrow pencil not orange lipstick.

"Do you have any more recent experience?"

She threw back her shoulders and narrowed her sharp, gray eyes. "No. I got married. We had two girls right away. My job was to raise them. I've outlived my parents, two brothers, and my husband. My daughters think I need a keeper. Always reminding me to brush my teeth and wash my face. I'm not a child, and I refuse to be treated like one."

Definitely not a child, she couldn't be much older than eighty. I wondered if her daughters knew she was traipsing around in public clad in her designer PJs and a single strand of pearls.

"Do you live in Laguna?" I asked.

"That's an asinine question. Where else would I live? Do you live in Laguna?"

I chuckled. "For a few years now. I haven't seen you around."

Her shoulders visibly relaxed. "My cat died ten years ago. I live with my oldest daughter. She doesn't like pets, so I don't have a reason to come in here. Until now."

"But you want to work here?"

She waved her hand in the air. "Sure, why not? You need help, and my daughter wants me out of her hair." She pointed a thin, wrinkled finger at me. "I think we can help each other out."

I was about explain she lacked the experience I needed when Tova Randall bounced into the shop upset.

"Melinda?" she called out in a shaky voice.

"By the coffee bar." I smiled at Betty. "Sorry. This won't take but a second."

Tova made a beeline for me, tissues wadded in her fist. "Melinda. Do you have a minute?" she croaked, tears in her voice.

"Does it look like she's got a minute, tootsie? She's about to hire me," Betty said wryly. "Zip up your shirt before you catch a cold."

I coughed back a laugh. I enjoyed Betty's spunk.

Tova fingered the zipper of her blue, velour jogging suit. Suddenly, she froze. Her red puffy eyes huge. She pointed at Betty's face. "You have —"

I jumped up, sending Betty's application floating to the hardwood floor. "Tova, I'm in the middle of something. Can you come back?"

"This is important." She sniffed, dabbing her runny nose, looking at Betty's eyebrows, horrified.

I picked up the paper. "What I'm doing is important too." I glanced at Betty, who was giving me a Grandma Tillie look. It was the same don't-disappoint-me look Caro and I got when we were trying to one-up the other.

"It's about Jack." Tova's voice was barely above a whisper.

"I'll meet you at the Koffee Klatch in thirty minutes."

Tova couldn't stop staring at Betty. "Okay. Thirty minutes."

I ushered Tova out the door, Betty right behind me. Once Tova was gone, Betty leaned close and said, "She's had a boob job. I can tell. She's one of those high-maintenance types like my oldest daughter. You really going to meet with her?"

Great. Even Betty thought I was an idiot. "Yes." Once I handed Tova Dr. O's last gift, hopefully I'd stop feeling guilty for being difficult last night.

Betty nodded and straightened her pearls. "Then you need someone to watch the store." She clapped her hands together and headed for the counter. "Let's call it a trial run. I know I'm cranky, but I'm honest, hard-working, and loyal, too. If you don't like the way I handle the place, you don't have to hire me. If I pass muster, the job's mine. Do you have an apron or a name tag?"

It was only for an hour at the most. How

much trouble could Betty Foxx get into?
Besides, once her daughters realized she was
loose, I had a feeling Betty'd quickly find
herself on a short leash.

"Do you have a problem handling cash?"
I asked.

# CHAPTER ELEVEN

I was momentarily insane. That's the only plausible explanation. If Betty hadn't distracted me, I wouldn't have agreed to meet Tova. I'd only get myself deeper into the trouble that swirled around her. Instead, I could have had a courier service deliver Dr. O's gift. Better yet, I should just refund it to Dr. O's credit card and put the booties back on the shelf.

I popped over to Darby's studio and filled her in on my temporary employee and my meeting with Tova. Darby agreed — I'd lost my mind, but I was doing the right thing. She also promised to keep an eye on Betty. Then I ran home to let Missy out.

By the time I arrived at the Koffee Klatch, the place was full of regulars. Tova and Kiki had found a spot on the purple overstuffed sofa. Kiki nibbled on a dog treat while Tova, who had zipped her top, stared bleakly out the picture window. There was a small pile of used tissues stacked haphazardly on the table in front of her. Eew.

I grabbed a chai for fortification before joining them. I took a deep breath then dropped on the couch with a sigh.

"Here." I held out the blue Bow Wow bag.

Tova faced me, her perfectly sculpted face serious. "Why did that lady have lipstick on her eyebrows?"

I rubbed my temple. This meeting was going to be a chore. "I don't know. It didn't come up. Take the bag. He wanted you to have it."

"I know. I told you that last night." She set the bag on the floor by her feet without looking inside.

"You did. I'm sorry I was so stubborn last night. I'm also sorry about Doc." I genuinely meant it, even if my tone was business-like.

She shredded a clean tissue. "Thank you."

I inhaled deeply, reaching for patience somewhere deep inside. "So, you mentioned something about Doc," I prodded.

She smoothed her hair with a shaky hand. "I know you and I aren't exactly friends," she started.

I gulped my tea, burning my tongue. I pried the lid off to cool it quicker. "No, we're not. But I have a bad feeling that's not going to stop you from asking me for a favor."

Kiki finally noticed me. She abandoned her treat and bound across Tova's lap to greet me.

"Hi, girlfriend. How ya doin'?" I scratched behind her ear as she licked the air around my face. She was one cute pocket-puppy.

"Are you and that Detective Malone friends?" Tova's soft breathy voice barely reached me.

I smiled at the absurdity of her question. I'm sure Malone called me many names. "Friend" was not on the list. "No."

"Oh. I thought since you helped him with Mona Michael's murder, that you two were, I don't know . . ." she motioned absently.

"BFFs? Not likely." I set my cup on the table. "Tova, What do you want?"

"There's a photo of Jack and me on Balboa Island in his office. I want you to help me get past that barracuda office manager of his so I can get it. I deserve it."

Maybe her eyes were red from something other than crying. "Have you been drinking?"

Tova flinched. "What? Of course not."

I couldn't believe it. She wanted me to cover for her while she stole from her dead boyfriend's office. Of all her non-friends, why did Tova Randall want my help?

I stood, ready to get the heck out of Dodge. "I don't think so."

"Is this because of the lawsuit?"

Yes. "You accused me of infecting Kiki with fleas. You threatened to sue me if I didn't reimburse your costs. Tova, bless your heart, you're crazy."

Tova grabbed Kiki and stood too. Her little dog wiggled in protest. "Wait. I've told you, I'm sorry about all that."

I stared at her in disbelief. "No. You've never apologized."

She had the decency to blush. "Well, I'd give you back the check, but I've already cashed it. Fifteen hundred dollars doesn't go very far these days."

I looked around. No one was paying us any attention. "You're the one who came up with that amount, which I gave you. Kiki didn't get fleas from Bow Wow," I reminded her.

"I know. I'm sorry. I am truly sorry." Tova's green eyes stared at me in earnestness.

Good grief. Who knew I was a sucker for a decent apology? I was getting soft.

"Melinda, please, just come to his office with me," Tova begged quietly.

"Why can't you go alone?"

"I've been to his office. It's closed."

That kinda made sense, him being dead and all. "Closed forever?"

She shook her head "Jack recently brought on a second surgeon. I think he called him a junior partner."

Tova motioned for me to sit again. I was rooted in place. I knew the smart move was to walk out of the Koffee Klatch and go back to the shop. But that nosey part of me wanted to know more. Plus I felt sorry for Tova.

I sat back down.

Tova shot me a million-dollar smile and returned to her seat too. "I stopped by Jack's office this morning to retrieve the photo. The door was locked. Gwen Lawson, the office manager, could see me through the glass doors. She just ignored me, pretended I wasn't there."

I wished I could pretend Tova wasn't here. Sitting next to me. Begging for my help. "Tova, I know you're upset. Doc . . ." I decided to drop the formality. "Jack was their boss; they're upset too. Give them a couple of days. I'm sure they'll let you in, and you can get whatever it is you want, assuming he has no relatives who have to be consulted, first."

"This can't wait," her breathy voice rose. "Gwen hates me. She's always hated that

Jack and I were together. She made up stuff to keep him away from me." Tova's mouth was set in determination.

I didn't want to help her. My rejection must have been obvious, because she kept pleading.

"That is all I have left of Jack. Pictures. The day I gave him that photo was the day he told me he loved me for the first time. It's the only copy. Gwen will relish throwing it away. If you were me, you know you'd demand that photo."

I rubbed the side of my face and sighed. She was right.

"You're going to keep asking for my help until I say yes, aren't you?"

She nodded, eyes hopeful. "Yes, I will."

I'd already experienced Tova's stubborn doggedness when she wanted something. It was draining. Last time I eventually paid her off to get her out of my hair. I could feel myself relenting.

"Tell me *exactly* what you want me to do."

"Just go there with me. They'll let you in. Talk to Gwen about Jack. Ask her questions, whatever you want, while I sneak to Jack's office to get the photo. It'll take five minutes. I promise if you help me get my picture from Jack's office, I won't bug you anymore."

"Ever?" My eyebrow arched until it disappeared under my bangs.

She nodded enthusiastically. "Yes."

She was seconds away from bouncing up and down in her seat like an excited preschooler. There was no way she could keep that promise.

"What time do they open tomorrow?"

She shook her head. "It has to be today," she insisted. "The office is closed Saturdays. Can't we go now? They close in a few hours."

After deliberately replacing the top on my tea, I stood and grabbed my drink. "I'll help you, but on my terms. If you don't like it, that's fine with me. I'll happily walk away, and you're back on your own."

"Okay. Whenever you say."

"I'll meet you there in an hour."

Tova jumped up, scaring poor Kiki. "Thank you."

"Don't make me regret this."

What was I thinking? The minute I hopped into my Jeep, I regretted agreeing to help nitwit Tova. I had a feeling my impulsive nature was about to get me into trouble. Again.

# CHAPTER TWELVE

Before I popped over to the studio to talk to Darby, I wanted to check on Betty. Granted, I'd been gone for less than an hour, but I felt badly I hadn't given her any real training other than a brief explanation on how to run the cash register and credit card machine. I'd also pointed out the bathroom in case she wanted to freshen up. Or fix her eyebrows.

When I got to the boutique, Betty insisted she was fine. She'd certainly kept busy. Somehow, she'd managed to find the last box of Christmas decorations in the back room.

Blinking colored lights hung precisely from numerous shelves, Santa hats perched on the heads of select dog and cat statues, and a Christmas tree, decorated with a combination of traditional ornaments and moderately priced collars, bows, toys, and other merchandise, stood off to the right.

Somehow, Betty had managed to create garland from dog leashes. Every customer would have to pass the tree to reach the register. It was genius. Her retail background was a gold mine.

Confident the store was in capable hands, I let Betty know I'd be next door for a few minutes then darted over to the studio, where I found Darby alone.

Her last session had ended. She bustled around the studio, putting away her props. I rushed over to help her with a large basket of pet toys.

"Weren't you wearing a dress earlier?" I asked as we shoved the heavy basket onto the metal shelf.

"I changed into jeans for the photo shoot with Shar Summers. I wanted some outdoor shots of her and Babycakes. You would have hated it." She laughed. "They wore matching pink sweaters and boots."

Shar had a bad habit of dressing her Chinese Crested in over-the-top outfits that matched her own — fur, feathers, or Swarovski crystals, it was all fair game. I guess she thought it was cute to dress like her dog.

Darby threw a couple of pillows at me. I tossed them next to the basket.

"There's been a slight change of plans

with your cousin's photo shoot. Caro requested we do it at her place, tomorrow morning at ten. It's easier on the cats."

As Darby dragged a ficus tree across the cement floor to the staging area, I racked my brain for a quick fix. "Can you talk her into a few shots here or outside maybe? Just her and Dogbert? On the beach or at the dog park? Anything to get her out of the house for an hour."

She brushed off her jeans. "We can't be too obvious. She knows I feel partially responsible that she has the pin again. I was so busy watching her case the boutique, I didn't think about watching the brooch. If I push too much, she'll know something's up."

I picked up the handful of scattered leaves and tossed them in the basket. "It wasn't just you. Heck, my eyes were glued to her too." Caro never came into the shop. At least not since we'd stopped talking to each other.

"Before I forget, I met Betty," Darby said.

I checked my cell. It was time to head over to Dr. O's office, but I wanted to hear her opinion on my almost part-timer. "What do you think of her?"

Darby worried her bottom lip. I could tell she was searching for the right words. "She's interesting. Seems to have a lot of energy."

"She finished putting up the Christmas decorations while I was out."

Darby nodded. "I wondered about that. You may want to consider reviewing your products with her. She tried to convince me the pale pink polish would look good with my skin tone. Does she understand you sell pet products?"

I laughed. "She used to sell cosmetics." I checked the time again.

"Are you late for an appointment?"

"You're never going to believe this, but Tova asked me to help her get a photo from Dr. O's office."

Darby pursed her lips. "You're right. I don't believe it. Why would she think you would help her?"

I shrugged. "Who can explain Tova? She thought Malone and I were friends."

"Where would she get that idea?"

"You know, because I 'helped' him once, so that must mean now we're best buds."

"She obviously doesn't know Detective Malone."

"Trust me, she wasn't going to stop hassling me until I agreed to run interference for her. She's so desperate, she apologized about the fleas."

"So what?" Darby narrowed her sharp

blue eyes. "An apology is easy when she wants something. She didn't have a problem spending the hush money you gave her."

"Whoa there, Tiger. First, it wasn't hush money. It was cheaper for me to pay her off than to fight a nuisance suit. I hate to acknowledge this out loud, but as annoying as Tova may be, between her and Jack O'Doggle, they've spent ten times that amount at my shop in the past month."

"You do remember Detective Malone said to stay out of it."

I smiled wryly. "I hear his droning commands in my sleep. Look, I'm running interference for Tova so she can grab a photo of her and the doctor. That's it. I swear. If you're that worried she's taking advantage of me, feel free to come along."

I'm not sure if Darby tagged along to keep tabs on Tova or me. Either way, I was glad to have her as backup. At three-thirty, we entered Dr. O'Doggle's office building in Newport Beach. It was as if we'd walked into the Montage Resort Hotel. The office exuded a specific lifestyle of sophistication, luxury, and money. He definitely catered to an upscale clientele.

Tova had changed into skinny jeans, a Stella McCartney colorblock print top, and black, four-inch pirate boots. I hadn't realized I should have dressed for the occasion. Darby and I were still in our everyday jeans and tops.

Not surprisingly, Tova hadn't followed directions. She'd arrived before us and, instead of waiting, barged inside and provoked the staff. It was a Charlie's Angels standoff. Three long-haired beauties in white shirts and black slacks against a lingerie supermodel. My money was on anyone other than Tova.

"I said, what are you doing here?" The tall redhead stepped away from the trio. She had to be the office manager Tova had complained about. What was her name? Oh yeah, Gwen.

Tova huffed. "I don't trust you. I came for the photo of Jack and me." She wasn't as confident as she tried to appear. Her hands trembled as she stroked Kiki.

"Hey, Tova," I called brightly as Darby and I walked across the room. With each step, my boots sank into the thick, white carpet. The handful of patients in the waiting room watched the group of women with intense curiosity. So much for not making a scene.

Darby and I reached the reception desk. Gwen could easily take Tova. It was obvious from her flexed stance that she knew her way around a bar fight or two. She was as scrappy as she was beautiful.

"Melinda, take Kiki." Tova shoved her dog at me then marched toward the back of the building. Her heels clicked with determination on the expensive tile leading toward the offices and examination rooms.

"You can't go back there." Gwen stomped after her.

"I knew this would go badly," Darby muttered under her breath.

I cradled Kiki, caressing her absently. "Sorry." I apologized to the duo of gorgeous women on the other side of the humongous mahogany desk. "I'm sure you know Tova can be a tad out of control." I made an effort to keep my voice low so the patients didn't overhear.

"Are you her friends?" Blatant distrust was apparent in the blonde's icy voice.

"Hardly. I own Bow Wow boutique. Tova's a customer."

"Oh," the girls said simultaneously. Two sets of earthy brown eyes transformed from suspicion to sadness.

"You found Dr. O'Doggle's body." That was the brunette.

"Ah, yes." I immediately felt uncomfortable. Darby was right. This was a bad idea.

I hadn't thought about their reaction to me. Was it too late to leave?

"I'm Bailey, the practice's Image Expert. This is Heidi, she's our receptionist."

"I'm Darby. I was with Mel when . . ." she trailed off.

"We're really sorry about your boss," I told them. "I'm sure this has been difficult for all of you." I held Kiki a little tighter. She licked my hand, as if knowing all of us needed comfort. Dogs were amazing creatures.

"It's been the worst," Bailey said. "Poor Heidi's dealt with constant phone calls all day. The police were here questioning us. O'Doggle's patients have been frantic about their appointments. Dr. Stolzman refuses to close. He doesn't want to get behind schedule since he'll inherit a number of O'Doggle's patients. Gwen finally locked the doors for an hour this morning so we could have a break and come up with a plan for the day."

That must have been when Tova showed up the first time.

Bailey dabbed teary eyes. "Everyone who works here loved O'Doggle."

I had to wonder if they'd still feel that way if they knew he didn't like dogs.

"He was an amazing doctor." Bailey's

voice broke. She swallowed hard. "He did all of our work." She indicated her face.

I had to admit, it felt like we'd walked into a plastic surgery slumber party. Large lips and larger breasts at every turn. I wasn't a self-conscious girl. Heck, the beauty pageant circuit is no cakewalk, but even I felt the need to stand a little taller among these women. If you know what I mean.

"And now she's back." Heidi scoffed.

"You don't like Tova?" Darby asked.

"I've worked here for five years. He's had a number of girlfriends, but he never spent the kind of money on them like he did on her. Boxes arrive weekly. Gifts for Kiki, gifts for her. Dresses, make-up, shoes, jewelry. Even a couple of wigs."

Jealous much, Heidi? I could see Tova with extensions, but a wig? "Are you sure about the wigs?"

"It was written right on the box," Bailey offered.

"I think he was getting ready to dump her." Heidi leaned closer and lowered her voice. "They used to have a standing date every Sunday night, but I know for a fact he broke the last three."

"How do you know?" I asked.

"I heard them arguing about it a couple of days ago."

Bailey shook her head in disagreement. "I don't think so. He was always trying to make up with her. Why else would he buy all those gifts? He could have done so much better." She sighed.

Like dating you, instead? It was written all over both of their faces. They were in love with their boss, which made them suspects in my book.

"Are you sure they were gifts for Tova? Is it possible he bought them for someone else?" I asked.

"O'Doggle told us they were for Tova," Bailey insisted.

Heidi narrowed her dark eyes. "Hold on. Now that you mention it, he never said Tova's name. He said for his special lady. We assumed he meant Tova."

Darby leaned on the desk. "Did you notice him acting differently lately?"

"What do you mean?" Bailey asked.

"Agitated? Secretive? Depressed? Scared?" I felt like Malone. Probably a clue to stop the questions. But Tova hadn't returned, so I kept the conversation alive. Just doing my part.

"No. He seemed really happy lately," she admitted grudgingly. "The business is really successful. He hired Dr. Stolzman a couple of weeks ago, after we started losing patients because we couldn't get them appointments quick enough."

Darby and I shared a look. Losing or stealing?

"I heard a rumor there was some type of lawsuit. Did that have to do with some other surgeon stealing Dr. O'Doggle's patients?"

Their friendly demeanor vanished. I'd gone too far.

Heidi set me straight with a drop-it-or-you'll-wish-you-had look. "I don't know what you're talking about."

It was time to leave. Tova had been gone way too long. I passed Kiki off to Darby and excused myself.

Finding Tova was simple. I followed her grating voice.

"You don't know what you're talking about. He was not cheating on me. He was going to propose." Tova sounded on the verge of tears.

"Propose? Are you serious? If this crap isn't for you, then for who? Face it, he had another girlfriend," Gwen taunted.

"He wasn't like that. You're wrong." Tova rushed past me with a huge, ugly, blonde afro wig clutched in her hand. I swear that wig could have walked on its own. Where had she found it? And why was she taking it with her?

I poked my head into the office. Gwen stood next to a large cardboard box, victory blazing in her hazel eyes. I looked around, absorbing as many details as possible. I had a feeling this was the only opportunity I'd get to see the office.

"You missed her." Gwen strode toward me. "She left without her prized possession."

I took the picture frame she shoved at me. "Is she okay?"

"She's fine now that she's been brought down to size. She needs to face the facts. He wasn't that into her." Gwen shut the door behind us and ushered me back to where Darby waited.

Judging by the picture Tova claimed, I'd have to disagree. They seemed happy. A candlelight dinner, both of them smiling into the camera as if they didn't have a care in the world. It didn't add up.

"Do you really believe he cheated on her?" I asked.

Gwen looked at me with a confident smile. "There've been rumors swirling for weeks. A couple of days ago, I found a tube of glitter lip gloss in his desk drawer. It's not Tova's brand."

Something in her eyes led me to believe she knew what she was talking about. It was almost frightening. I couldn't prove it, but I had a hunch Gwen knew exactly who that lip gloss belonged to. And she wasn't sharing her information with me.

# CHAPTER THIRTEEN

The sun was setting, cueing a colorful end of an even more colorful day. I pointed the Jeep south. We bounced along PCH, back to Laguna, each lost in our own thoughts. The radio played quietly in the background, a female voice reciting the top news. I heard Dr. O'Doggle's name and quickly turned up the volume.

"The police have confirmed the death of renowned plastic surgeon, Jack O'Doggle of Newport Beach. His death has been officially classified as a homicide. Dr. O'Doggle's body was found in front of the Bow Wow Boutique in downtown Laguna Beach yesterday morning. The cause of death has not been —"

I turned off the radio. I'd heard enough.

After the latest news bulletin, it struck me that we may have unwittingly helped the killer dispose of incriminating evidence. I felt sick to my stomach. I know, too little too late.

"I really hope there isn't an eyewitness out there who saw a woman with a hideous blonde afro leave the scene," I said.

Darby's breath hitched. "Do you think someone on the doctor's staff killed him?"

"I don't know. If someone did see something, Tova's the only one carrying that ugly wig around town."

I kept my eyes on the road. Traffic slowed as more cars filled the highway. I switched lanes to pass a black SUV with Montana plates driving well under the speed limit. Visitors. Ugh.

"Should we tell Malone?" Darby asked.

"Tell him what? Tova's acting like a crazy woman, running around town with a blonde afro wig that shouldn't ever be worn? Not even for a Halloween slasher movie?"

"That about sums it up. Are you going to call or shall I?" Darby asked.

The light at the Crystal Cove State Park turned red. I stopped the Jeep and contemplated what to do about Tova and her wig.

"It doesn't prove anything. We have the picture, which was supposedly the whole reason she went there in the first place. She'll be back. Let's talk to her then."

Darby looked at me, her face suddenly sympathetic. "Do you think he was cheating on Tova?"

I shrugged. "Gwen thinks so. She knows more than she's divulging. If there is another woman, we need to find her. Maybe she's the one who killed Tova's cheating boyfriend."

"We?" Darby squeaked. "I think we need to stay out of it."

The light turned green. I accelerated, heading for the boutique. My thoughts collided with possibilities. If Jack O'Doggle really was strangled with a dog leash, were any of those women strong enough to kill him? Was he killed in front of Bow Wow or was that a dumping ground? Either way, why in front of my shop? Did it mean anything or was it just coincidence?

Staying out of it. A nice thought.

Execution was a different matter altogether.

Twenty minutes later, we were back at the boutique. The bell jangled our return. Other than Betty bustling around the shop, the place was empty.

"It's Melinda," I called out before I flipped the sign to Closed. "How'd it go?"

"Slow. You need to come up with some ideas to drum up business." She turned to face me. When she saw Darby her eyes lit up. "Hi, there. Change your mind about the nail polish?"

Darby smiled. "Afraid not."

"Your loss." Betty shuffled to the counter, her sneakers squeaking on the hardwood floor.

As she got closer, I could see she'd refreshed her lipstick. Only on the lips. Maybe the eyebrow thing was a fluke.

She picked up a yellow notepad. "You had a couple of calls, tootsie. Vera White inquired about the job. I told her you'd filled the position." She shot me a denture-filled grin. "You should send her an official rejection letter. She seems like the needy type." She licked her boney finger and flipped the page. "A Detective Malone called. Said he was still waiting for a list of addresses. He'll be at the station late tonight."

Darby sent me an uneasy glance. My heart skipped a beat. I'd forgotten about the addresses.

"You didn't mention where I was, did you?"

Betty shrugged a fragile shoulder; her silk pajamas slid forward, showing off her extra-white skin. "He didn't ask."

Darby elbowed me. I knew what she was saying. Close call. We joined Betty behind the counter and shoved our purses on the shelf.

"Did you help that lady get her photo?" Betty asked.

I pulled the frame out of my purse. I looked at it with a critical eye. It didn't look like it was anything special. Gold, five-by-seven, a burgundy felt backside.

"She left in a rush and forgot to take it with her." Which meant I'd have an opportunity to talk to Tova again. Boy, did I have a lot of questions.

Betty picked up the frame and smiled. "They look happy. My Tommy gave me a picture frame just like this many years ago. I miss him sometimes." Her fingers traced the gold beveled edges.

"I'm sorry, Betty. How long ago did he die?" Darby asked softly.

"Ten years ago this Thanksgiving. Died of a heart attack at the family dinner table. Face plant in the mashed potatoes and gravy. Kplat! Never saw it coming."

"That's awful." Tenderhearted Darby patted Betty's arm.

"Once the family stopped laughing, we realized he was dead. The girls were devastated. We had some good times, me and my Tommy." She handed the photo back to me.

"You never remarried?" I asked.

"I love an attractive man, but I don't want to be hitched to another. Unless it's for lovin'." She wiggled her faded eyebrows. "Do you know any good men, cookie?"

Darby's lips pressed together, hiding a smile. I blinked rapidly, working hard to not picture Betty's definition of lovin'. Too much information.

"I'll have to think on that," I said.

"Did you check the secret compartment on the backside?" Betty's face softened. "My Tommy used to hide notes for me. He was a romantic."

A secret compartment? I flipped the frame over. A small tab, just big enough to hold between your thumb and index finger, stuck out, begging to be pulled. It wasn't exactly a hiding place. It was how the back came off to insert the photo. But I could see how someone might hide a note behind it if they were so inclined.

I pulled the tab. A newspaper clipping fluttered to the counter.

"What'd I tell ya, cookie?" she cackled.

I unfolded the paper. It was an advertisement for opening night for an entertainment show. The venue name was missing. I didn't recognize either of the women in the picture. They weren't exactly natural beauties with their enormous hair, sequined gowns, and a ton of eye glitter; they posed in a manner that was neither natural nor sexy. The headline read Jackie O and La—a. La—a? I wasn't even sure how to pronounce her name. I decided to go with "La-ah".

Could one of them be the "other woman" we had heard about?

"Let me see." Betty tugged on my sleeve.

I showed it to her and then Darby.

Betty scrunched her lips disgusted. "Blondie needs a new hair stylist. Her hair is awful. It looks like a wig."

I chuckled. It did look like a wig. Exactly like the wig Tova carried off to God knows where. My pulse quickened. I blinked, making sure I was seeing what I thought I was seeing.

"That dark-haired one looks familiar. I've seen her before." Betty tapped her nose in concentration.

"I don't think Tova knows about this," Darby stated.

"You're thinking what I am, aren't you? That's the wig Tova stole."

"I remember," Betty shouted, her petite body vibrating with excitement. "They're drag queens. I saw their show at the Kitty Kat Club. That blonde, Jackie O, she was bad. No timing, bad makeup. Came out in a pink suit and pillbox hat. Horrible. I got my money back."

I completely avoided the fact that Betty had been to a drag show. "You're sure?" The blonde did have a strong jaw line.

"I'm old, but I'm not on my deathbed. You girls need to get out more. Experience life. Those aren't ugly ladies. They're definitely drag queens."

I looked closer at the photo. Something clicked in my brain. "Oh. My. Gosh." You could have knocked me over with a feather. "Jackie O is Jack O'Doggle."

# CHAPTER FOURTEEN

The Kitty Kat Club had a reputation for over-the-top fun and bawdy humor. I'd Googled the club and found their website in seconds. There was a show tonight at eleven. It had taken some cajoling and begging, but I'd finally talked Darby into going with me. It was decided that I'd pick her up at ten.

Then I called Betty's daughter, Valerie. After a brief chat, I realized why Betty wanted out of the house. Valerie seemed fixated on her need to be the center of attention rather than her mother's need to keep active. I hired Betty to work four hours Monday through Friday.

I told her to come back the next day at noon for some official training. That would give me time to run a background check, too. You never know.

After Betty and Darby had gone, I printed out the addresses I'd promised Malone and ran them over to the police station. For once, luck was on my side. Malone was otherwise occupied. I left the report with the clerk and skedaddled before my luck ran out.

I loved adventure and new experiences, but even I felt apprehensive about tonight. On the drive home, I racked my brain for anyone who might have some pointers. Then it came to me. The perfect person was right under my nose.

The minute I opened my front door, Missy greeted me with snorts and kisses. I loved her up and told her I missed her. While I filled her dog bowls with water and kibble, Missy found her leash and dragged it to the kitchen.

"You wanna go for a walk?" I scratched her head with all the adoration I felt for my pooch. "Okay, let's go." I grabbed my cell and off we went.

While we were on our walk, Darby called to let me know Caro had agreed to a few outdoor shots. I promised to be at Caro's by nine forty-five the next morning.

Once Missy was finished with her doggie business, inspecting every bush and tree along the route, we returned home.

I pulled my cell from my back pocket and

called Kendall Reese, groomer extraordinaire.

"Divine Dog Spa," a female voice answered.

"Hi. This is Melinda Langston. Is Kendall there?"

"Hold on a minute." I heard her set the phone down. Dogs barked and howled in the background as I waited.

I dropped to the couch and pulled off my boots. I'd met Kendall a couple of months ago and immediately enjoyed his flamboyant personality. If anyone knew their way around a drag club, he had to be the one.

"Kendall here," he said with poise and professionalism.

"Hey, it's Melinda Langston. I have a huge, huge favor to ask."

"Girlfriend, if this is about Fluffy, forgetaboutit. That doggie doesn't like me." His feminine voice, full of Latin attitude, filled my ear.

I was pretty sure there was a hand-wave and snap that I couldn't see at the end of that sentence.

"Snob Dog doesn't like anyone. Don't take it personally. I called because my friend and I were hoping you'd come with us to the Kitty Kat Club tonight? You know, show us the ropes."

"Ooooh. Are you gettin' your inner diva on?" he asked excitedly.

I smiled. "Something like that. What do you say? Are you in?"

"Sounds fab-u-lous."

I looked down at my jeans and T-shirt. "One last question. What do we wear?"

Kendall had two syllables of advice. "Spar-kle." Snap.

I decided on my black Rachel Zoe sequined shift dress and t-strap gold pumps. I pinned my hair into an intricate updo with sideswept bangs. A little something I'd learned during my pageant days. Darby kept her hair down and wore a more understated navy Michael Kors number and nude platform shoes.

"Yoo-hoo, Melinda. Over here," a sing-song voice clamored above the music.

For a second I thought I was trapped in a bad music video. A tall, wiry man Soul Trained across the crowded floor in tight, black tuxedo trousers and a red lamé shirt unbuttoned to his wide waistband. Kendall had his own style, but tonight he'd outdone even himself.

A handful of gold chains slapped his hairless chest as he boogied closer. The second I was within reach, he grabbed my hand and twirled me in front of him.

"Oooh, Mama, you look hot, hot, hot."

He swiveled toward Darby and tsked dramatically. "Girlfriend, where's your sparkle?"

She held up her gold sequined clutch, apparently afraid to speak. I was under the same spell.

"My sad little doggie has more sparkle than you," he said with a head bob. "You need to loosen up with some alcohol. Follow me ladies." And off he danced.

The club was huge. To the left, a separate dance room, packed from mirrored-wall to mirrored-wall with gyrating bodies and throbbing bass.

To the right, the bar. It had to be the largest bar I'd seen since college, stretching the full length of the wall. It was crammed with a handful of men and tons of women. All dressed to kill, willing to battle it out for a beer or martini.

I have to admit, I was slightly disappointed. The Kitty Kat looked like every other club. Low lights, blaring music meant to prevent meaningful conversation, and a miniscule sitting area. Oh, and plenty of drunks.

Kendall chatted up our fellow partiers, inching us closer to the front of the line.

Finally, we ordered our drinks and were ready for the show.

"Where's the best place to sit?" I shouted at Kendall.

"Right up front, honey." He pointed toward the stage straight ahead.

I'd totally missed it. In my mind, the stage should be larger. In reality, it was barely six feet wide, framed by blue velvet curtains. I tipped the bartender a few bucks, then we made our way toward the stage.

Once again, we followed Kendall. There were a handful of empty tables left. We claimed the closest to the stage.

"It doesn't look any different than the bars in Nebraska." Darby's blonde curls bobbed as she looked around. "It's really loud," she shouted. Darby hadn't drank an ounce of her rum and Diet Coke.

"Did you bring your dollars?" Kendall sipped delicately on his champagne cocktail.

"Sure did. Why do we need them?" I asked.

"You'll see." Kendall's lip-glossed smile spelled T-R-O-U-B-L-E.

I drank my dirty martini as I watched a boisterous bachelorette party crank up the fun with Jell-O shots.

At exactly eleven o'clock, the lights dimmed and the music climaxed. Spotlights flashed the audience. Black spots danced before my eyes.

A faceless voice boomed from the speakers. "Are you ready to be swept away by the queens of the night?"

The mob roared in response. If I looked half as terrified as Darby, we were in some serious trouble.

"Give it up for . . . Miss . . . Bea . . . Haven."

The screaming crowd rushed the stage like a Longhorn steer stampede. Was there a fire? My heart pounded in time to the music.

The curtains parted, and Jennifer Hudson's doppelganger appeared. I swear on my family's good name she looked right at me and smiled. Jennifer glided from one end of the stage to the other, lip-syncing perfectly to "Love You I Do," from the movie *Dreamgirls.*

Her silver and black beaded gown shimmered in the light, casting a spell on the audience. She stretched her arms toward the crowd, accepting (or encouraging, depending on your point of view) countless dollar bills thrust in her direction.

"I thought these were men?" Darby looked confused.

"They are," Kendall patted her arm. He

whipped out a five from his wallet, answering the siren call. "Isn't she delicious?" He waved his money in the air as he shimmied toward the edge of the stage.

Each time Jennifer accepted money, she air-kissed her admirer's face. The crowd ate it up, begging for more.

"That is not a man," Darby argued. She removed the straw from her glass and gulped her cocktail. Her eyes watered. "Mel, those are real breasts."

I shook my head. I'd seen enough chicken cutlets in my day to know even the best breast can be faked. "I don't think so. His . . . ah . . . her makeup is perfect, though. If he didn't have an Adam's apple, I would have never known he isn't a woman."

This was Dr. O'Doggle's secret life?

Maybe Tova had a motive to kill her boyfriend after all. She didn't strike me as a woman willing to share the spotlight with a female impersonator. I doubted she could handle the competition. After all, he was cheating on Tova.

With himself.

The show lasted little more than an hour. The highlight was when Cher emerged from behind the curtain in her iconic black feather headdress and slayed the crowd with her rendition of If I Could Turn Back Time. Buzzed, Darby had yanked a dollar from her wallet and shoved her way to the stage. She'd even managed to evade the required butt slap from the drunk dude up front. Sometime after Cher's air kiss, Darby switched to water. Probably a good idea.

The lights were back to I-think-you're-sexy-but-I-can't-see-you-clearly-to-know-for-sure, and the music had been toned down to a decibel where conversation was somewhat possible. Needless to say, I had a bucket full of questions, including a few about Dr. O'Doggle.

"Do you know how much skill it takes to look that good?" I asked Darby and Kendall. "We all know some women who could take a lesson from these guys."

"No, no, no. When they are in drag, they are ladies," Kendall explained.

Darby clutched a half-full bottle of water. "I still can't believe they were all men. Are you certain?"

Kendall smiled, pleased with our reaction to the show. "Positive."

"Even the one wearing the electric blue cat suit?" she asked.

He nodded. "All of them." Kendall explained the proper way to "tuck."

Darby shook her head. "Amazing."

"They'll come and mingle with us in a few minutes." His Latin accent thickened the more he drank. "Do you want to meet a special one?" he asked Darby. "Cher, maybe?"

"I don't think so."

"Is La-ah here?" I asked, finally remembering the reason we were there in the first place.

Kendall shot me a funny look, but before he could answer, the drag queens started to appear. Each one had changed into new costumes. I couldn't recall a time I'd seen so much spandex and glitter, evening gowns, boas, and elbow-length gloves. Cat suits and go-go boots floated throughout the room. Each queen wore glitter on her face. Eyelids, lips, cheeks. It felt like a pixie dust party.

The High Priestess of drag queens paraded toward our table in her black spandex cat suit and cape. Her body was amazing. Her fiery red wig was striking. The closer she drifted to our table, I could see her mocha skin glistening with perspiration.

I was fascinated with her makeup. Singular swipes of dark blush emphasized high cheekbones. Dramatic blue-green eye shadow enhanced her black eyes. The exaggerated strokes took a trained, steady hand.

117

She was good. And judging by the predatory look on her face, she knew it.

"Kendall," she cooed in a surprisingly feminine voice. Dark lip liner drew attention to her full lips, to which she'd applied glitter gloss.

Could she be the owner of the mysterious lip gloss Gwen had found?

"Introduce me to your friends." She batted caterpillar lashes as she dragged her fingers through his hair.

He swatted her hand away good-naturedly. "Don't be naughty. Melinda, Darby, this is Goldie Fawn. Goldie brings her Chihuahua, Miss Kitty, to Divine Spa."

"The show was very entertaining," Darby said.

"Thank you, dah-ling. I'm thrilled you enjoyed yourself." She pointed a deadly gold fingernail in my direction. "You look very familiar. Where do I know you from?"

Since he — she — had a dog, I went with the obvious. "I own Bow Wow Boutique."

Her plump smile faltered. "That's right. I bought Miss Kitty's new green lead from you."

Darby's head whipped in my direction faster than the Linda Blair scene in The Exorcist. I kicked her under the table.

"You must have paid cash. I'm sure I

would have remembered you," I said with a smile.

Her laugh was definitely male. "I don't wear drag in the daytime. It's a little scary, even for me. Ladies, it was decent meeting you."

Decent? Did she just insult us?

Kendall grabbed a handful of her cape. "Where's Ladasha? Melinda wanted to meet her."

I'd been pronouncing the name wrong. La—ah was Ladasaha.

Goldie pinned me with her peacock eyes. "Why?"

It would take more than a good smoky eye to intimidate me. "I heard she performed with Jackie O."

"You know Jackie? Are you a friend?" All pretenses of femininity evaporated.

"Would that be a bad thing?"

"I don't like that bitch. She thought she was better than us. So, yes, it would."

Kendall stood. "I'm sure Melinda didn't mean to upset you."

There were times the direct approach was best. This was one of those times. "Jackie O was murdered. Darby and I found her in front of my boutique. We just wanted to ask Ladasha some questions."

"Move over." Goldie shoved Kendall aside

and stole his seat. "What are you talking about?"

I opened my clutch and pulled out the clipping we'd found. "This is her, right?"

She neither denied nor confirmed. Instead, she scorched me with her stare. "I haven't heard anything about a dead drag queen."

"When we found her, she was a he. Dr. Jack O'Doggle, the plastic surgeon. Do you know of anyone who wanted to hurt him? Her?" Now I was confused.

Kendall on the other hand was about to have a meltdown. "I did not know. I promise." Sweat seeped through his shirt.

Goldie stood. "Don't move." She sashayed away.

"You tricked me. Why would you do that?" Kendall wailed.

Good grief, he was an emotional mess. "We didn't trick you. We didn't know about Dr. O'Doggle's other persona until six hours ago. I wasn't even sure I believed it completely. Until now."

Kendall rubbed his face. "What have you done?"

Within minutes, Goldie Fawn came back flanked by Jennifer Hudson and Cher. A drag queen gang? "Come with us," Goldie ordered.

Darby said quickly, "I don't think that's a good idea." Her blue eyes were huge.

"Neither do I." Damn. I was wearing four-inch heels, hardly the right shoes for fighting or running. "I didn't come here to cause problems."

Goldie pointed at Jennifer. "This is Jackie O's drag mama. And she" — Goldie pointed at Cher — "is Ladasha."

I'd fallen down the rabbit hole. Drag mama? "O-kay. We can't talk out here?" Where there are a hundred witnesses? I didn't care if I had to strain to hear. We were safe in the open.

Jennifer said grimly, "We could whoop your skinny ass here and no one would stop us. In fact, most of these people would help. We" — she swept the room with an arm — "are a family. If you want answers, you'll come with us." Jennifer's soft voice brooked no argument. It was her way or not at all.

Okay then. Guess I was about to be educated.

# CHAPTER FIFTEEN

Kendall bailed. Something about not leaving his Pomeranian, Guido, an orphan. The bartender called him a cab, and off he went. Honestly, I was relieved. I couldn't concentrate during his hysterics.

We didn't go far. Down the hall, to the right, and into a private room. The air was stale and smelled like day-old beer. The only place to sit was a loveseat that should've been tossed to the curb three decades ago.

Darby and I sat side-by-side. No sense in dragging it out. Pun intended.

"Did Jackie ever explain why she decided to become a drag queen?" I asked as delicately as possible. I tried to show respect for a community I didn't understand.

Bea Haven hovered over us. The feathers from her boa tickled my nose. "Normally, I have a drink in my hand before an interrogation."

"Normally, I'm threatened with jail," I

muttered. Darby elbowed me. "What? It's true."

"No. Jackie never opened up about why. Being a drag queen is a visual art. We're entertainers," Bea said.

"Is that why you do it?"

"My reasons are my own. I don't get personal until at least the second drink. Look. We all have our motivations. Some want fame. Others want to look on the outside the way they feel on the inside. You have to be tough to stay in this business for any length of time. The competition is fierce."

I could relate. Beauty queens were equally conniving but not as open about their intentions to take down whomever they perceived as competition. At least drag queens were up-front.

Bea turned to Goldie. "Why did you bring us back here? There's nowhere to sit. I'm tired, and my hand is still empty."

"We needed privacy, and this was it. Stop complaining, you old bag. You've been drinking like a fish all night. The other room is occupied."

I shuddered. I didn't want to know what the other room had that this one didn't. "We're happy to let you sit down."

Darby nodded. "Absolutely."

"Then get your skinny asses off that couch."

She didn't have to order us twice. We scrambled off the loveseat, making room for the others.

Bea and Goldie sat. Ladasha watched all of us silently as she rolled down her black gloves, revealing hairless arms, then pulled off the gloves one finger at a time. She was still performing.

Bea kicked off her size-twelve platform heels and rubbed her feet. "Man, that feels good. I hate these shoes, but they're just so damn sexy."

"What's a drag mama?" I asked.

"An experienced drag queen who takes a newbie under her wing and shows them the ropes. Gives them pointers. Helps them with their makeup," Bea explained.

Recalling the photo of Jack, he needed a mama. His makeup was atrocious. He did not understand the concept of blending.

"And you were Jackie O's drag mama?"

"I've been in this business twenty years. I am the only drag mama these ladies have ever known."

"Was he any good?" Darby asked.

Goldie laughed cruelly. "He was awful."

"I thought you'd made nice with Jackie?" Ladasha finally spoke.

Goldie flashed her pearly whites. "I was faking it."

I turned to Ladasha. "Did you know him well?"

Of all the queens, she seemed to take Jack's death the hardest. And by that, I mean she was the only one not talking smack. She shrugged. "We performed together for a few months."

"Did he have any enemies?

"Come out with it, girl. What you're really asking is did any of us kill him." Goldie said.

I raised my eyebrow daring her to answer.

"We may throw shade at each other —"

"Pardon?" Darby finally found her voice.

"Shade. Trash talk. It's an art form, and not all drags are good at it. But for those of us who are, that doesn't mean we'd kill each other," Bea explained.

"Jackie rested on pretty. You can't just be beautiful. You have to have talent." Goldie flipped her hair. Obviously, she was talking about her amazing talent.

"Somebody thought she had talent," Ladasha said.

Goldie jumped up. "Shut up. Ain't nobody asking you to talk about that."

"I am," I said. "What do you mean?"

Ladasha's narrow fingers shook. "Jackie deserted us to sign up for a reality show about a group of new drag queens coming up through the clubs. If you want to know what happened to her, you need to talk to the producer, Danny Stone."

"Great. Where do I find him?"

Goldie rolled her eyes. "Girlfriend, you're dumber than a beauty queen. L.A., of course."

I slept in. I don't normally sleep past eight, but I was so exhausted after all of last night's excitement, I must have needed the rest.

I took a quick shower then walked Missy around the block a couple of times before putting on my breaking-and-entering clothes. Black jeans, T-shirt, and hoodie. It was cooler than normal this morning, and like every winter day, the fog blanketed our oceanside town. I slipped on my leather jacket for extra warmth. After pulling on my boots, I headed out the door. My heart raced in anticipation as I mentally walked through the plan to retrieve my pin.

I parked a block down the street from Caro's place. My fingers patted my pocket, double-checking I had my copy of her house key. I was thinking about where I'd look first when my cell rang. It was Darby.

"Caro's wearing the brooch." She sounded

panicked.

"Where are you?" My stomach twisted at the unexpected complication. Why hadn't I thought of that? It's exactly what I would have done. Dang, Caro!

"Heisler Park."

"Make her take it off," I demanded.

"How?"

"I don't know. You're the photographer. Make her take it off and put it in her car."

She fumbled with the phone. "Here she comes. I gotta go."

I started the Jeep. Dang, dang, dang. I hit the gas. My tires squealed around the corner. I had to come up with a plan, fast. I drove to the shop. It was only a few blocks to the park. I'd walk. I didn't want to spook Caro if she accidentally saw the Jeep.

I pulled my hair into a ponytail and yanked the hood of my sweatshirt over my head as I scanned PCH for Caro's vintage silver Mercedes. I spotted it next to a black Caddy Escalade and a Prius. I sighed. This wasn't going to be easy.

There was no sign of Darby or Caro. I jogged to Caro's car. Locked. I lay on the ground and looked under her car for a spare key. I felt behind the tire well. Sure enough, I found a small metal box. I pried it from its hiding place.

I stood, brushed off my jeans, and tried to act nonchalant, in case anyone was watching. My heart beat in my chest so hard I thought I'd have a heart attack. I unlocked the driver's door and slid behind the wheel. The interior was perfectly clean. No fast food wrappers, water bottles, or to-go coffee cups. It even smelled clean. Gawd, she was such a neat freak.

I checked the glove box first. Owner's manual, tire gauge, and a pen. Next I looked in the door-side pockets. Empty. I felt under the driver's seat. Nothing. Under the mats, between the seats, and in Dogbert's carrier in the backseat. Disappointment threatened to overtake my excitement.

I was about to give up when I accidentally slid the seat back a few inches. I felt around. Nothing. I shifted to the passenger side and repeated the search. Bingo. As soon as my fingers touched a handkerchief, I knew I'd scored. That's when my cell phone rang. Crapola.

I yanked it from my pocket. Mama. Lordy, she had the worst timing.

"Hey, Mama. This isn't a good time." I returned the seats to the original positions.

"It's never a good time for me to call you, Melinda Sue. I'm calling about Christmas. It's three weeks away. Are you coming like you promised your brother, or are you breaking your daddy's heart this year too?"

"Mama, please don't guilt me." I quickly scanned my surroundings for unwanted company. "I'm kinda in the middle of something right now. I'll call you later. Give Daddy my love."

I ended the call and scrambled out of the car. Once it was locked up as tightly as I'd found it, I returned the key to its hiding place.

The second Caro knew I had the brooch, she'd be more dangerous than a rabid dog. I ran like hell back to the boutique, pumping my fist in the air like Rocky, before she could catch me.

I'd won.

# CHAPTER SIXTEEN

Saturday morning flew by. So did Caro's Mercedes. She was a professional and had finished the photo shoot with Darby quickly, but I'm sure the pictures were going to show her steely side. Darby was suffering from duplicity remorse. She was just too soft-hearted for her own good. I hoped she never changed.

There'd been a steady flow of customers for the first couple of hours. Some of them even made a few purchases. Mostly, there was a lot of small talk about who could have killed Dr. O'Doggle and if I really thought Tova was involved. You know, it's hard to stay out of Malone's business when every-one else keeps bringing it to my doorstep.

It was twelve-fifteen. Betty was late for our special training. I'd just picked up the phone when I heard the front door open. I set it back on its charging station.

"There you are. I was getting worried." I

turned around to find myself staring at the shortest female version of a drag queen this side of Arizona.

"What do you think?" Betty struck an awkward pose. Wrapped in a royal purple evening gown, boa, and elbow length gloves, you knew she'd channeled her inner diva for inspiration. A handful of feathers fluttered to the floor. Good news. The only lipstick on her face was in the right place. "Your sneakers gave you away. I think you have too much time on your hands. Why in the world are you dressed like that?"

"I planned on surprising you and Darby last night, but I fell asleep in my chair before the ten o'clock news. You girls wore me out. I need to make sure I take my vitamins." She stroked a blonde wig that had to be from the Reagan administration.

I thought about all the drama. Thank goodness Betty hadn't been with us. Who knows how that would have played out.

"If you're still playing detective, I can go undercover. Those dames got nothing on me."

Riiight. Other than a couple feet and triple-D cutlets. "I think we're good. Are you wearing that getup all day?" If she didn't stop the hip action, she'd end up in the ER.

"Nah. I got a change of clothes in my handbag. I'll be right back."

Betty scampered toward the bathroom. I shook my head. I could only hope I had that much energy at her age.

The door opened and in walked Tova and Stacie. Believe it or not, I did a double take. Tova looked awful. Unbrushed hair, dark circles under her eyes. Her stonewashed jeans and shirt hung on her. She looked like the before photo for an anti-aging serum.

"Hi, Mel." Tova said softly. "I forgot to grab the photo from Jack's office. Do you have it?"

I pulled it out from under the counter. "Gwen made sure I took it with me."

She made a face. "I told you she hated me."

"Did they tell you anything about the new doctor? Was he stealing Jack's patients?" Tova's assistant asked.

Stacie seemed to be thriving under the stress. She looked refreshed and in charge. She drifted around the store as if looking for something. Interesting.

I noticed her hands were still red. "You need to have that rash looked at."

"It's fine," she insisted. "It'll go away in a couple of days. Well, did you ask?"

"It didn't come up. Tova, how well did

you really know Jack?"

Color tinged her pale face. "We didn't keep secrets. He was not cheating on me."

"I agree. With the cheating part. But he was keeping a secret." I handed her the clipping. "We found this in the back of the frame."

"You were snooping in my personal belongings?" she screeched.

Betty meandered toward the front of the store. "Oh, it's you. I thought someone stepped on a cat."

I choked back my laughter. "I wasn't snooping," I lied to Tova. "It fell out when I pulled the tab. What are you going to do, sue me?"

Tova froze. "No," she said in small and very unnatural voice.

Stacie began looking under display stands and along the wall. "Tova's been under a lot of stress. I would think you, of all people, would understand that."

"I would also think she would have learned to not attack those who were helping her. What are you looking for?"

"I thought I dropped an earring just now."

She was lying. I could see both earrings plain as day.

Tova stared at the clipping. "I don't understand. This was in the frame?"

I nodded.

Her hands trembled. "Why? Who are these people?"

Unease washed over me as I was about to destroy her perfect boyfriend world. "Jack and another man."

Both Stacie and Tova blanched.

Tova stepped back like a weaving drunk. "What are you saying, Melinda Langston?"

"Your boyfriend was a drag queen. He's 'Jackie O.' "

"You're lying." She wadded up the clipping and threw it at me.

I picked up the small paper ball. "Why in the world would I make up something like that?"

Stacie looked like she was ready to lunge across the counter and pull my hair out. "Because you're mean."

I couldn't help it. I rolled my eyes. Were we suddenly back in high school, and I was the mean girl? "That's it? Because I'm mean?"

Betty pooh-poohed her. "You sound like a yippy puppy. What are you going to do, piddle on her boots?"

As much as I enjoyed her zingers, Betty was not helping. I made a mental note to coach her on filtering her thoughts. I turned my attention back to Tova. "All those dates he canceled? He was performing. All the boxes of clothing and jewelry, they weren't all for you. That wig you ran off with . . ."

I let the implication hang in the room and slowly sink in. I wasn't sure who was going to throw up first, Tova or her assistant.

I walked to the coffee bar and poured them each a mug of water. "I met them last night."

"Who?" Tova called out.

I returned with their water. "Here. Drink this. We met the drag queens at the Kitty Kat Club."

She shook her head. "This can't be true. He loved me. We talked about getting married. He was cutting back from the office. He hired another surgeon."

"According to the ladies, he'd signed up to be part of a reality show about drag queens."

Tova's mug shattered on the hardwood. She continued to shake her head in denial. "I don't believe you."

"Stacie, take her home."

Stacie set the water on the counter, shooting me a nasty look. "Let's go, Tova. You'll feel better after a nap. I've got something that will calm your nerves."

Whatever Stacie was going to give her, it probably wasn't going to be enough.

■ ■ ■ ■

I loved Sundays. After a relaxing session of doggie yoga, Missy and I walked on the beach. We were in the middle of a game of tag when Grey called letting me know he was home. Missy and I were both excited.

I invited him to stay at my place, but he wanted to sleep in his own bed. So Missy and I would be enjoying a sleepover at Grey's. I grabbed a pizza from Gina's on PCH, and we drove the twisty streets to Grey's place in the highlands, otherwise known as The Top of the World. It was the best spot in town to experience the sunset.

I parked in Grey's driveway. Missy jumped out of the Jeep and hightailed it for the door. I grabbed the pizza, my overnight bag, and purse and followed close behind. The door opened, and there he stood. He looked delicious.

"Hey." I played it cool. What I really wanted to do was jump in his arms, but that was no way to treat a Gina's pizza.

He took the pizza box from my hands. "Hey, yourself. What's with the smile?" he asked.

"You're cute." I reached up and kissed him. He smelled clean. Man-soap clean. He must have just showered.

"You're not too bad yourself. Missy's already in the kitchen. Let's go."

"How was your trip?" I left my bag and purse in the living room and followed him.

"The bad guy got away." He set the pizza on the table next to a bottle of red wine.

I ignored the immediate anxiousness that bucked at my insides. "What does that mean? Will you have to go back?"

Grey and danger were willing partners. I hated when I didn't know where he was or exactly what he was doing. I didn't trust the unknown, which was partly why I tended to jump headfirst too quickly. I needed to know what I was up against. Not Grey. He liked subterfuge, developing a strategy to outwit his opponent.

Up until recently, if I even mentioned his undercover work, he'd change the subject. We'd agreed to have more faith in each other. He promised to share what information he could, and I'd promised to stop worrying about what I couldn't control. Some days it was harder than others. Personally, I preferred his cover life as an art gallery owner. At least then, I knew where he was. Plus he had a natural eye for great art.

He grabbed a couple of paper plates, and I grabbed the wine glasses. We quickly set the table.

"I'll have to go back eventually," he said.

"I'm sorry the target got away." I hugged him. He felt good. Solid. Strong. I closed my eyes and savored the moment.

Grey kissed the top of my head. "What about you? What's going on?"

I stepped out of his embrace and smiled. "I hired a part-time helper."

"Good. I can't wait to meet her."

"I have to warn you, she might try to steal you away. I have a feeling she's looking for a hook-up."

He looked at me questioningly. "I'm sure I can handle her."

My smile widened. "I don't think so. Ol' Betty's one of a kind. Promise you won't abandon me once you set eyes on her. She's pretty feisty. Sometimes she reminds me of Grandma Tillie."

He chuckled. "I'm not sure I can make that agreement. I think I need to see this Betty first. How's Darby?"

We sat at the table and dug into our dinner.

"Recovering," I answered around a mouthful of pizza.

"What does that mean?"

I washed down my food with a swallow of wine. "Well, Friday night we went to a drag bar. And yesterday I managed to get my brooch back from Caro." A meatball rolled off my pizza and onto my lap. I pushed it onto the floor in front of Missy, who had camped under the table for any falling scraps.

"Brooch first. It will take the least amount of explaining. Then I want to know about the club."

I explained the calendar, photo shoots, and how Caro thought she'd flaunt the brooch in my face by wearing it. And how Darby talked her into taking it off. He wasn't exactly proud of my duplicity, but he'd stopped fighting it. At least when it came to the brooch.

Then I mentioned the name of the drag club.

He shot a sideways glance my way. "Since when did you and Darby start hanging out at drag clubs?"

I wiped my mouth. "Don't get mad."

"I wasn't. But every time you start a sentence with 'don't get mad,' I automatically know I'm going to be mad."

"I'm trying to break you of that horrible habit." I leaned over and kissed him lightly on his nose.

"Is this about Jack O'Doggle?"

"Yes. Tova asked me to run interference

for her while she retrieved a photo from his office. She got sidetracked by an ugly wig and left without the picture. I brought it back to the boutique with me. Betty mentioned she had a frame just like it with a secret hiding place for love notes."

"So, naturally, you looked." His cheek twitched.

Uh-oh. The cheek-tic.

"Of course. Only it wasn't a love note, but an advertisement for a drag queen named Jackie O."

I let him digest what I'd said for a few seconds. "The doctor performed in drag?" he asked.

"Yes. According to his drag mama, he wasn't very good. But apparently there's a producer in L.A. who saw something interesting about him, because he hired Jack for a reality show about new drag queens."

"I thought you were going to stay out of this investigation."

"I am. I will." I placed my elbows on the table and leaned closer. "Think about it. So far, the police have no suspects other than Tova —"

"That you know of," he clarified.

"True. It could have been a number of people. Gwen, the office manager, Ladasha the moody drag queen, the office staff —

Heidi or Bailey — they were in love with him. Or it could even be the new doctor. Maybe he got greedy and wanted the practice all for himself."

Grey dragged his fingers through his hair. "Mel, you have to stay out of this. Last time you poked your nose into police business, you almost got yourself killed."

I smiled reassuringly. "But I didn't."

He leveled a look that shook me. He was about to explode. "You were lucky I was there to save you."

I straightened. "You did not need to save me."

"This is dangerous business. You have zero training. You act before you think, if you even think."

My chest constricted, pinning down my bubbling anger. I stood and dumped my plate in the garbage.

"First of all, asking questions is not dangerous, and I do not need training to do so. Second, I'm not involved. I plan on calling Malone first thing tomorrow to tell him about Dr. O'Doggle's secret life."

"And then you're done."

"Maybe." I took a deep breath and counted to three. "We agreed, no lying," I said, holding back a sigh. This was another sticky area in our relationship. I had issues with his dangerous job, and he had a problem with my inability to turn off my snap judgments and my penchant for meddling in police business.

"That doesn't make it okay to do what you want and discount how I feel." He tossed his plate in the trash.

"Hold on there. That's not what's happening."

"Isn't it?"

"Not at all. Look, you just got home. Can we change the subject? I love you." I shoved him toward the living room until he fell onto the couch. I jumped on his lap and wrapped my arms around his neck. "You love me."

He wasn't exactly melting in my embrace.

"I don't want to fight," I said.

He sighed. "I don't either."

I kissed his neck softly and whispered, "Good. Let's do something else. Welcome home."

I felt his muscles tense. "We're not finished discussing this, Melinda."

"I know," I said honestly.

He looked at me with an intensity that made my heart race. I searched his eyes for some clues as to what he was thinking. Then he slowly kissed me as if he'd missed me more than breathing.

# CHAPTER SEVENTEEN

The Koffee Klatch was the last place I thought I'd ever run into Detective Malone on a Monday morning. He struck me as the kind of guy who bought his coffee out of vending machines. No sweetener, no milk, and certainly no flavored syrup, just straight-up joe. Yet there he was, waiting in line like the rest of us gourmet caffeine junkies.

He placed his order and then stepped aside. By the time I'd ordered my usual, he'd paid up and left. Well, that's what I'd thought, anyway.

Surprise. He was waiting for me outside. I'm sure to the average passerby we looked like a pair of regular citizens, since both of us wore jeans, T-shirts, and black leather jackets. Who'd suspect he was a cop waiting to threaten an innocent woman with jail for merely asking questions?

"I got the addresses," he said after sipping

his drink. "Thanks."

His dual personality, Mr. Warm and Fuzzy, was in charge this morning. "You're welcome. Any news on who killed Doc?"

"If I didn't know better, I'd think you're getting involved in my investigation." He fixed me with The Look.

"Let's be honest. I'm involved whether I want to be or not. He died in front of my store. I helped you find potential suspects by giving you a list of names and addresses."

"How do you know he died in front of your store?"

That caught me off guard. How did I know? "I just assumed. Are you saying he didn't die there? That someone dumped him?" I wasn't sure how I felt about someone purposely choosing my business to dump a dead body.

Malone studied me for a full second. "We're following the evidence."

We moved to the sidewalk, out of the way of the Koffee Klatch's customers. The sounds of morning traffic competed with our conversation.

"So there is evidence? Besides Tova's bracelet. Because, I've got to tell you, I'm not sure she's the one. Do you have fingerprints or DNA?"

His eyes narrowed. "You're not that involved."

Too late. I took a sip of chai. "Did you walk here?" I asked.

"Why?"

"I have something to tell you, and I need to get to the shop. Can you talk and walk?"

He nodded in agreement, but the look on his face clearly stated he was anything but agreeable. The brisk morning air stung my cheeks. I huddled underneath my jacket as I searched for the least annoying way to share my information.

"Do you know how he died?" I asked.

"Not your business."

I could hear shoes slapping the cement behind us. I stepped aside and let the runner pass. Malone waited for me to catch up. I matched my step with his. "What if I told you he had a secret life?" I asked.

"On the Internet?"

"Better." I wasn't doing a good job of hiding my enthusiasm. I waited to continue my story until the bus passed us. "Darby and I were doing Tova a favor and, in the process, learned Jack had an alter ego."

"Get on with it, Melinda," he said pointedly.

"Dr. O was a regular performer at the Kitty Kat Club. He was a drag queen."

He missed a step. "What?"

Was that real surprise on Malone's face? That was all the encouragement I needed.

"You never know about people, right? His fellow drag queens thought he lacked talent. Get this. His stage name, Jackie O. He even did one number in a pink suit with a pillbox hat. Kinda creepy, if you ask me."

Malone nodded at an older couple walking their beagle past us. Once they were out of earshot he asked, "How do you know all of this?"

"We found a clipping in a photo frame he had on his desk and thought we should check it out. We asked around . . ." I trailed off as I realized I was sharing more than I needed to.

"Who did you talk to?"

"Goldie Fawn. Bea Haven. Ladasha That's spelled L and then a dash and then just the A."

Malone stopped in front of one of the many art galleries in town and looked at me, unimpressed. "What are you talking about now?"

"They're drag queens. They've all performed with her, uh him. Miss Bea Haven does a mean Jennifer Hudson impression. Seriously, dead on. Her makeup is amazing. And boy, do those girls have attitude. I'd suggest buying Bea a drink if you want the real skinny on Jackie O. She wasn't all that helpful for us."

"You went to a drag show?"

"Me, Darby, and Kendall Reese. He works at —"

"I'm well aware of who Kendall Reese is."

I'd bet my last dollar there was a story there. "If the subject comes up don't mention this to Caro. If my mama got wind, she'd hop on the first plane to the OC."

"You dragged Darby with you?"

I was offended. "I didn't have to drag her. She offered to go." Okay, that was a fib. She didn't offer to go, but I certainly hadn't dragged her, either.

"Probably to keep an eye on you and Kendall. She's the only level-headed one in the bunch. I'll check out the story. You keep out of it. Understand?"

"You might want to take backup. You're pretty good-looking. Have you ever seen drag queens fight for man-candy?"

"I can't say that I have."

I swear his shoulders were shaking. I couldn't tell if he was laughing at me or shuddering at the thought of being fought over by men dressed as women.

"Go alone, and you'll get a front row seat."

"I'll keep that in mind."

It wasn't until I was back at the shop that

I realized he hadn't threatened to throw me in jail. Things were looking up.

# CHAPTER EIGHTEEN

I sent Betty to pick up our lunch at the deli down the street. She wanted a grilled cheese. That sounded like a fine choice until she explained what the gourmet deli put on it — pickles, marinated onions, and tomatoes. I'd stick with my plain old egg salad sandwich, thank-you-very-much.

The door chimed. I looked up from organizing the bark-mitzvah collars and caught my breath. Vera White was back.

I should have sent that letter like Betty suggested. Darn, this wasn't going to go well. Vera wore a surgical mask and had her antibacterial sanitizer in her hand.

"Hello, Vera. I'm sorry I haven't gotten back to you yet."

"I know you've hired someone. I called." She eyed the white collar I held. "I came to tell you I couldn't take the job anyway. I found out I'm allergic to dogs."

Ah, the reason for the mask. "That's too

bad." I hung the merchandise and crossed toward her.

"Not really. I didn't like dogs anyway." She pulled out a box of exam gloves from her doctor's bag. "Even though I won't be working for you, I haven't stopped thinking about your shop. I brought you these as a gift. Would you like me to bring you some sanitizer?"

"Actually, I bought some." I pointed at the bottle on the counter.

Her dark eyes beamed. "Good." She held out the box of gloves. "I haven't slept since last week. My therapist said it's because I'm obsessing about your lack of sanitation. Please. Take them. I need to rest."

It was difficult to tell if she looked exhausted with half her face covered, but her wiry hair looked a little flat. I accepted the gift. Who was I to keep her from sleeping? "Non-latex," I noted.

She nodded. "Just in case you're allergic and don't know it. You can never be too careful."

"Thank you. I'll keep them behind the counter."

She balled her hands. "You've put up more decorations since I was here."

I was about to tell her it was Betty's handiwork but thought better of it. "Hopefully it helps to put my customers in the holiday spirit."

"Be sure to dust everything before you pack it away. It cuts back on the germs."

"I'll keep that in mind."

After wishing me luck, she pulled out a package of disposable wipes and used one to open the door on her way out.

Yowza. I tossed the gloves under the counter and promptly forgot about them. Once I'd sorted and arranged a display of bow ties and veils to my satisfaction, I high-tailed it back to my office. I wanted to review that list of names.

Goldie Fawn had been here for the Ava Rose event. Why hadn't I asked for her real name the other night? I was sure Kendall knew, but he wasn't exactly talking to me. He was still angry that I failed to mention Jackie O. I strolled to the front of the store, list in hand. Was Goldie a Michael? Lars? Ben? Ramon? Kevin?

"Melinda? I need your help." A soft, strained voice broke my concentration.

Startled, I jumped, tossing the paper in the air. I hadn't heard the bell, yet there stood Tova. Without Kiki or Stacie.

She didn't look any better than she had on Saturday. She'd thrown on a jogging outfit and white sneakers. The shoes were a red flag. Tova wore heels with everything. Dark circles still hung under her eyes like mink coats. The poor gal looked like ten miles of Texas back roads. That was not a compliment.

"I didn't hear you come in." I picked up the paper, folded it into a square, and shoved it in my back pocket. "Where's Stacie?"

Tova shook her head. "I don't know. With her brother, I think."

Well, she needed to get back here pronto. Tova needed a keeper. "I didn't realize she had family here. What's he do?"

"He's an actor or something." She fingered a doggie trench coat on the wall.

"What can I do for you?" I kept an eye out for Betty, who was due back at any time.

Tova listlessly drifted through the store, avoiding eye contact. "Detective Malone came by my house today. He told me to get a lawyer."

Well, there's a conversation starter. "He must have some pretty strong evidence." I led her toward the coffee bar.

"My bracelet. The one I wore to your party. I thought I lost it here. The clasp was loose. I meant to take it to the jeweler's to be repaired. I hadn't gotten around to that."

The bracelet had to be what Stacie had

been looking for. Only it was too late.

"It was under Jack's body." I poured myself a mug of hot water and tossed in a lemon.

"I didn't kill him," she insisted, her voice growing stronger. "Gwen knows something about his death."

I, too, thought Gwen was hiding something. "Why are you so sure?"

I offered her a mug, but she declined. "Jack said she was sending his patients to another surgeon."

"That's a pretty serious accusation."

She ran a shaky hand through her stringy hair and paced in front of the dog carriers. "He was going to confront her Wednesday night. That's why he wasn't coming to your party. He said he found proof."

"Did he tell you what kind of proof?"

"No. He didn't have a chance."

"Did you tell Detective Malone about this?"

She whipped around, her green eyes wild. "Yes, but he only cared about my alibi. And when I last saw Jack. What we talked about. If we fought. He asked very personal questions."

Unfortunately, that's how it was done. "Do you have an alibi?"

"Of course." Her shoulders sagged. "Well,

I thought I did. After your party, Stacie and I went to my place and worked on my upcoming schedule. Malone said that wasn't good enough. Jack was killed early in the morning. I was alone then. I told him to ask Gwen where she was at the time, but he didn't seem to care."

Time of death. Malone had kept that to himself. I wondered what else he hadn't shared. Not that he had to share anything with me. We weren't partners.

"Did he mention DNA or fingerprints?" I asked.

"Nothing. According to my lawyer, there's nothing concrete to put me at the site of the murder. I can't believe I'm asking, but will you talk to Jack's staff again? See if you can find out what evidence he had?"

I shook my head, sympathetic to her plight, but I wasn't the right girl for the job. "Have your lawyer talk to them."

"I didn't kill Jack."

"Then let the police do their job. Malone will follow the evidence."

"I don't want to go to jail. What'll happen to Kiki?" Tova rushed to the front door and locked it.

"What are you doing?" I chased after her.

"I want to tell you something, and I don't want anyone to barge in and interrupt me."

I sighed. Good grief. What more was there to say? She was innocent. She loved Jack. Blah, blah, blah.

"What I'm about to tell you has to stay confidential," she urged.

"I'm not your priest or your shrink. Are you sure you want to do this?"

"Melinda Langston, you may speak your mind, but I know you're a fair person. And I sure as hell know you can keep a secret."

She knew me pretty well. "Fine."

"Pinky promise?" She held out her right pinky.

Strike that. Not well enough. "Don't push it."

Tova straightened her shirt and cleared her throat. "Thank you." She took a few deep breaths and closed her eyes for a couple of seconds. Then she cast a forlorn gaze toward me. "I haven't always been beautiful."

I blinked. Was she serious? "Uh-huh."

"I've had some plastic surgery."

Okay, now I wanted to laugh, but I held back when I saw the seriousness in her face. "Tova, I don't want to hurt your feelings, but that's not a secret."

"I'm not talking about breast augmentation. I had my first surgery at ten. For my ears."

Of course I looked at them. Who wouldn't? They appeared natural to me. She had a good surgeon.

"I was tall and gawky. A real klutz. My ears were huge. My nose too big for my face. I had a mole on my cheek." She rubbed her face absently. "I had bushy eyebrows. I started waxing at eleven."

To look at her now, that was all very hard to believe. She had flawless skin, a delicate nose, and perfectly shaped eyebrows.

"I was teased horribly as a child."

Her hollow tone grabbed me. "I'm sorry," I said automatically. I truly was. No one deserved to be bullied or teased. Especially a child.

She batted away my apology. "I was called the usual names. Dumbo and elephant ears. Mostly by my mother. She thought she was toughening me up. She was tired of me running home after school crying like a big blubbering baby." She let out a heavy sigh. "I loved my mother, but she loved to make fun of me."

Whoa. No, no, no. I did not want to relate to her. If there was anything I understood, it was the insane, push-pull-love-hate mother-daughter relationship. I stomped the feelings of empathy bursting inside of me.

"After my mother paid for my ears, she

156

moved on to my nose and mole; she even convinced the surgeon to do a chemical peel on me, so my skin tone would be perfect. By the time I was sixteen, I'd had five surgeries."

Who does that to her child?

"But look at you now." I attempted to stay positive. I didn't want to deal with a crying Tova.

"Yes, look at me. My mother died in a car accident when I was twenty. Now I make money on the face and body she paid for. The man I loved is dead, and the police have me listed as the prime suspect. I didn't kill Jack."

I was doomed. My black heart ached for her. I felt her distress, and I hated it. I'd fought those same battles with my mother. Of course, my mama wasn't dead. She was just in Texas.

Suddenly, I understood Tova. Hell, that was a bitter pill to swallow.

"Malone is fair." Lame, I know.

He was also stubborn and unforgiving if lied to. Plus, he showed a propensity for tunnel vision, but I didn't think now was an appropriate time to share my insights.

"Tova, if you're hiding anything from him, he'll find out. It's better to be up-front. Now."

"I'm not hiding anything," she insisted. "Help me."

"How do you think I can help you?"

"You helped clear Darby's name. Help me clear my name, too."

"Look, Malone specifically told me to stay out of his investigation."

"I'm sure he's told you that before."

"He has, but that time was different. Darby's my —" I caught myself.

"She's your friend." She finished flatly.

I felt a little ashamed. "Well, yes. She is."

"Just talk to Jack's staff. You have a way of getting information from people. Please."

I don't know why I hesitated. She'd had me when she said her mother called her Dumbo.

"Have you ever heard the name Danny Stone?" I asked.

She nodded. "I think so. Maybe he was a newer patient of Jack's? I met him once at the office. Why? Does he know something?"

Before I could answer, Betty showed up, banging on the door. She wore a red silk outfit and pearls. She held up a bag containing our lunch.

"I have to let her in." I unlocked the door. "Sorry, I didn't realize it was locked," I fibbed.

"You can't make any money if you lock

the door, Melanie."

"Melinda." Why couldn't she remember my name?

"I'll just call you Cookie. Here." She pushed the bag into my hands. She brushed past Tova. "You look terrible. I thought you were some famous model. You should take better care of yourself."

"Let me know what you find out." Tova scurried out the door and down the street before I could say a word.

# CHAPTER NINETEEN

After lunch, I phoned Mama. Between her earlier inconvenient call and Tova's sob story, the guilt I normally ignored had developed into a demanding blister of regret. Turned out, I was wallowing in a bowl of sorry for nothing. At least where my mama was concerned.

Come to find out, mama was playing Mitch and me to get her way. My brother, an architect based in Las Vegas, specialized in luxury hotels. Two weeks ago his firm had dropped a new project in his lap, which meant he and Nikki were headed to Dubai for Christmas. Mama erroneously thought if I promised to spend the holiday in Texas, Mitch would beg his bosses to postpone the trip.

What Mama didn't realize was that Mitch probably asked to spend the holidays in Dubai. Thanks to my brother, I was off the hook. I'd make sure to send him and his lovely bride a box of their favorite candy as a thank you.

I'd also phoned TV producer Danny Stone. It was easy enough to find him with a simple Google search. Not so easy to see him. I left my name with the receptionist at his production company, but I had little hope she would actually relay the message. I even mentioned it was about Jackie O, hoping to prompt a return call.

A couple of teen girls drifted into the shop. Betty greeted them with a loud hello and immediately directed them toward the nail paw-lish. They giggled over the names, keeping Betty occupied.

I'd been thinking about Tova's situation. There was so much to remember. I had a difficult time sorting everything I'd learned over the last couple of days. I pulled out a note pad and started a list. It looked something like this:

Jack lived on Balboa Island/worked in Newport

Didn't like dogs (ask Tova about that one)

Plastic surgeon/drag queen

Hired new junior partner

Was recently hired for the cast of a reality show about drag queens

Was murdered in the a.m. before dawn

Suspect left no fingerprints or DNA evidence

It didn't seem like much to work with. I thought about the suspects and grouped them together on a new page.

### Suspects

Public life: Gwen, Bailey, Heidi, Dr. Stolzman, Tova

Secret life: Bea Haven, Ladasha, Goldie Fawn, Danny Stone

It was time to find out who else knew about his secret life.

Betty refused to let me close the shop. She swore she'd be fine while I ran my errand. I think she was worried I was losing money and couldn't pay her. I didn't bother correcting her about my finances. I wasn't the type of person to announce to the world I had money. Honestly, it wasn't anyone's business.

Shortly after three, I arrived at Dr. O'Doggle's office. Or was it now officially Dr. Stolzman's office? Something to think about.

Once again there were patients hanging out, flipping through magazines, waiting for a nip here and a tuck there. Or for some, a completely new face. I zipped past the wannabe Barbies and headed for the reception area. As luck would have it, Gwen, Heidi, and Bailey were all there, chatting away like gossipy teenagers.

"You're back." That was Gwen. I knew she wouldn't be happy to see me. She'd pulled her long auburn hair into a sleek ponytail, making her face look more severe than usual.

"I learned something I thought you should hear in person," I said.

"Well, let's hear it," Gwen challenged.

Heidi bounced in her chair. "Tova's been arrested?"

I shook my head. "No. This is about Dr. O."

"Tell us," Bailey begged.

"He wasn't cheating on Tova, but he did have a secret."

All three exchanged looks. Gwen seemed uneasy. The other two, mostly curious. Watching them reminded me of a Grandma Tillie saying, "It's easier to let the cat out of the bag than to put her back in it."

I positioned myself so I could see all three faces at once, praying someone would give herself away as the killer. "Have you heard of Jackie O?"

"No," Bailey and Heidi said.

Gwen shook her head, remaining silent.

"She's Dr. O'Doggle's other persona." I paused for dramatic effect. "He was a drag queen."

The two girls gasped.

"And he was about to star in a reality show about drag queens."

Gwen flinched then hissed. "Keep your voice down."

"Who's a drag queen?" a deep male voice asked. It belonged to a handsome man dressed in blue tailored scrubs. He appeared straight off the pages of People magazine's Sexiest Man Alive issue.

He had to be Dr. Stolzman.

"O'Doggle," Bailey sighed, practically licking her lips. "Melinda was filling us in."

Once again, I held everyone's attention. I continued, keeping my voice lowered. "The wigs, lip gloss, clothing. They weren't for Tova at all. Everything was for him."

"Why did he want to be a drag queen? He wasn't gay," Heidi said.

Dr. Stolzman leaned against the desk next to Bailey. "It makes perfect sense. With plastic surgery, you have one foot in science and one foot in art. He'd mastered this art form. He was looking for a new medium."

Stolzman was a little too quick to find this all agreeable. "Sounds like you know a lot of drag queens?"

"Actually, I do. Plastic surgery is a tight community. Before I came here, I practiced in L.A. I've worked on a number of drag queens. Many of them very famous. They're serious about their craft. If they can correct even the slightest imperfection, they will. Especially those who impersonate celebrities."

"So you did what type of surgery exactly?" I asked.

"I specialize in facial procedures, the same as Jack did."

I pointed to the crowded waiting room. "His death doesn't seem to have slowed you down."

He shrugged. "I don't have time to indulge sentimentality. This is a competitive business. If you want to be successful, you must work hard and sacrifice. I've got a duty to keep the practice going. I'm not going to hang a wreath on the front door and shut down for a period of mourning. Jack brought me in as a junior partner, but our contract allows me to buy out his share in an unfortunate circumstance like this, so now I'm running the show."

Wow. Dr. Stolzman just took top billing as suspect number one.

Gwen turned a scathing look on me. "If you're here to imply that one of us had something to do with O' Doggle's death, forget it. It was Tova. She must have learned about his hobby and killed him in a fit of disgust and humiliation. Maybe she wanted to stop him from doing the reality show."

Tova wasn't exaggerating about Gwen hating her. "I'm positive Tova didn't know about his secret life."

"Well, then, the killer must have been one of those drag queens," she said with a flip of her hand.

"It had to be a man," Dr. Stolzman said grimly. He kept his voice low, glancing at the waiting room to make sure no patients seemed to be listening.

"Why?" I said. All four of us turned toward him.

"Jack worked out every morning at Jim Chow's Fitness for Life Gym. It takes a lot of physical strength to perform certain surgical procedures plus plenty of stamina to get through long operations. Jack worked out with weights. He had incredibly strong arms and hands. There's no way a woman could have strangled him."

A good point. Doctor Hottie on the other

hand, well, his muscles had muscles.

"You mean the murderer must be someone like you?" I asked.

He smiled, flipping a chart shut. "Sure. But it wasn't me. I have an alibi."

I narrowed my eyes, pinning him down. "You don't even know exactly when he was killed."

"I don't have too. I'm never alone. Wednesday night I was in surgery with Jack. When he left, I had patient rounds at our recovery resort. From there I went home to my girlfriend. I was up at five and at the gym. With Jack, by the way. I left at six-thirty and was here by seven. Now excuse me, I have patients waiting." He flashed a cocky smile and then looked at Bailey. "Georgia Baker's ready for her forty-thousand-mile checkup. Can you set-up an appointment with her for photographing?" He oozed charm and sex appeal.

She nodded, wide-eyed, eating up the attention. "Sure."

Darn. I checked him off my suspect list. But I added that Jack was last seen at the gym at six-thirty.

"What about patient stealing?" I asked Dr. Hottie. "Were you and O'Doggle poaching patients from other surgeons? Maybe one of them was fed up with Jack's tactics."

Gwen positioned herself between me and Stolzman. "No one is stealing patients. I don't know where you heard that, but it's not true. You'll have to go now. We have work to do."

I knew I'd get nowhere as long as Gwen was within earshot. I had one last question.

"What about a disgruntled patient? I heard there was a lawsuit."

Gwen actually snorted. "That absurd lawsuit was dropped. A former patient's husband wanted to sue O'Doggle for conspiracy to commit fraud."

"That sounds serious."

"It wasn't. A couple of years ago, this patient came in for a complete overhaul. Lipo, lips, chemical peel, rhinoplasty, and a chin implant. A short time later, she meets this hot shot Hollywood producer. She never tells him how much plastic surgery she's had. They get married and start a family. He thinks she's cheated on him because their son doesn't look like either of them. Finally, she spills about her new face. He sues her for divorce and for fraud, claiming she misrepresented herself in order to get him to marry her. He dragged Dr. O'Doggle into it, accusing him of conspiring with her. The doctor had nothing to do with her plotting to snag a husband."

Wow. Just when you thought you've heard it all. I guess you can buy a new face, but you can't buy new DNA. Ouch.

I took my leave before Gwen kicked me out. Who knew, I might need to come back again. I walked back to my Jeep feeling I'd wasted an hour. I didn't have a lot of new information, and I had the same suspects I'd started with. Except for Dr. Stolzman. Obviously, he had been one of the last people to see Jack alive.

Speaking of Dr. Hottie . . . if what he said was true, about a woman not being strong enough to strangle Jack, my suspect list suddenly shrank in half.

# CHAPTER TWENTY

Grey was at Bow Wow with Missy when I returned. I'm sure his visit was twofold — to check on me and to meet Betty.

When I waltzed inside, I spotted Betty preening around the shop like a peacock. She'd even found some time to freshen up while I'd been out. Including her eyebrows, which were now Pretty in Pink.

Grey stopped talking and turned in my direction. "I thought I'd come in and introduce myself to Betty."

"I had no idea you had a fiancé, Mindy," Betty cooed.

That was it, I gave up on correcting her. "He's been out of town."

At the sound of my voice, Missy ran to me, leaving a trail of slobber in her wake.

Spin, spin, spin.

I bent down and greeted her. "Hey, there."

Grunt, snort. Grunt, snort.

"You're awfully happy today." I laughed

as she licked the air around my face, nailing my chin a couple of times. I rubbed in her doggie kisses, then dried my hand on my jeans.

She begged for a good scratching. I started behind her ears, working my way to her wagging hiney.

"She's missed you," Grey commented. He leaned against the counter, appearing relaxed in his jeans and sweater.

Finished greeting my dog, I stood and made my way to Grey's side. I greeted him with a kiss too. The scratch-down would have to wait. I smiled at him. "I see you two have been getting acquainted. Betty, would you toss me the paper towels under the counter?"

She batted her eyelashes at Grey as she handed me the roll of towels. "Handsome. And he owns an art gallery."

I quickly cleaned up Missy's mess before someone slipped on dog slobber. I tossed the garbage in the trash.

"What do you think?" I eyed Grey with a grin.

"I like your Betty."

"Oh, Mindy, you have a message," she interrupted. "Some guy named Danny Stone called. He said he'd be happy to talk to you, but he doesn't have a lot of time.

He could meet you at House of Joe in Santa Monica at six."

That was just over an hour away. "Thanks. Did he leave a number?" I didn't take my eyes off Grey.

"Nope. He said you had it."

If I was going to make that appointment, I needed to leave soon.

"Dinner tonight?" Grey asked. He may have looked relaxed, but he was on alert and gauging everything I said. But mostly what I wasn't saying.

"Yes. I really need to talk to Danny."

His square jaw line tightened. "This is about Jack?"

I nodded. I wouldn't lie to him.

"You know I don't want you to do this." His voice was tight; clearly he was frustrated with me.

"I know. I'll explain everything at dinner."

What I couldn't promise was that he'd like what I had to say.

I arrived early. I had no idea what Danny Stone looked like. When I'd called his receptionist to confirm, I briefly described myself (tall, brown hair, and brown eyes) and what I was wearing (jeans, sweater, and flats.) She didn't reciprocate.

I inhaled a savory java aroma. Why didn't

coffee taste as good as it smelled? I strolled through the shop, which had zero personality compared to the Koffee Klatch, waiting for Danny to call out my name. No such luck.

I ordered a drink, sat down, and waited. And waited.

I checked my cell for the third time. It had been twenty minutes. Had I misunderstood? Did I get the time wrong?

"Melinda?"

I looked up at a short, prepubescent, bald guy with mischievous green eyes. And an extra-large coffee. "Danny?"

He held out his hand. "You didn't tell Leslie you were beautiful. Are you an actress?"

I laughed. "No. I own a pet boutique in Laguna Beach." I motioned to the chair across from me.

"Have you ever considered television?" he asked.

Right. I longed for public mocking and overly harsh ridicule of my private life just to satisfy a bunch of strangers' warped sense of entertainment. Yeah, not interested. "No. I have plenty of crazy in my life. Thanks for meeting me."

"Sure. We were all surprised to hear about Jackie O. Did you know her well?" He pried off the coffee lid and dumped in four packets of sweetener.

"No. I knew her as Dr. Jack O'Doggle, the plastic surgeon. I didn't know about his other life until just a couple of days ago. I heard he . . . she," I quickly corrected, "was going to participate in your reality show."

He stirred his coffee. "Dr. 90210 meets RuPaul. Instant drama and conflict. It's too bad she wasn't murdered while we were shooting, that would have been a ratings gold mine."

Was my mouth open?

"Now we're stuck looking for a replacement. Have you talked to Jackie O's drag family? Maybe they know someone." He sipped his coffee, watching me over the paper cup.

The body was barely cold, and they were already replacing Jackie O. I ignored his question to ask one of my own. "Did Jackie O have any enemies?"

He shook his head. "Not that I know of."

"Where is the show set?"

"Right here in L.A." He gave an ironic laugh. "Funny how things work out. Originally we'd cast someone else, but then we met Jackie O and everything changed."

"So you fired the other performer?"

He nodded. "We had planned on replacing her. She didn't pass a psych test. Had a few personal problems that, even by our standards, might be too disruptive. We like 'crazy,' but only in a certain way."

"What kind of problems?"

He gulped his coffee. "I can't discuss that. Are you sure you don't want to be on TV? I've got this new concept I'm pitching —"

"Do you remember her name?"

"Sure. It's hardly forgettable. Ladasha. She spelled it —"

"L, a, dash, a."

He looked surprised. "You know her?"

"I met her recently. How did she take being fired?"

"Not well. She threw a chair against the wall, pulled off her wig, and collapsed on the floor." He shrugged. "Her histrionic fit was for nothing, since we weren't filming. She made a few more wild threats then left. She tends to be over-dramatic. I never did tell her she didn't pass her psych test."

In my limited experience, over-dramatic was a prerequisite for reality stars.

He slid his business card across the table. "I have to get back. If you change your mind and want to give Hollywood a shot, give me a call. I'm sure I can find something for you. I mean, come on, you pamper the pets of the stars. That's a good idea for a show, right there."

I tucked his card in my purse. I was sure Malone would want to talk to him. "I'll keep that in mind."

After Danny left without taking the last of his coffee, I knew what I had to do. It was time to go back to the drag queens.

# CHAPTER TWENTY-ONE

Ladasha killed Jackie O.

It all fit. She was already miffed about losing the reality show. When she'd learned she'd been replaced by Jackie O, a drag queen on training wheels, Ladasha flipped her eighties' Cher wig and strangled poor Jack with a dog leash. It made perfect sense, in a drag queen sort of way. Especially considering Dr. Stolzman's point about only a man being strong enough to commit the crime.

I couldn't prove any of it. That was Malone's job. But I could help.

Not to be deterred, I pointed my Jeep back to Laguna Beach. By the time I'd arrived at the Kitty Kat Club it was close to seven. The club lacked its glamorous appeal prior to show time. There was no pounding music seeping through the walls or flashing lights hypnotizing you to enter the garden of wickedness.

In other words, the place was closed.

I knocked for what seemed like forever. I was about to call it quits when a tall guy in jeans, a hoodie, and a knit beanie cap walked up behind me holding a key.

"What are you doing here?" He slipped a pink backpack off his shoulder.

I didn't recognize his face, but his slightly feminine voice was familiar. "I came to see you. Do I still call you Ladasha?"

Apparently, I'd asked a trick question because it took him a moment to answer. "David," he finally replied. "I'm only Ladasha when I'm in drag."

Again, I learned something new. "Do you have a couple of minutes?"

He unlocked the door and walked inside. I squeezed past the closing door, hot on his heels.

"You ask a lot of questions. You're sure you're not with the police?" He eyed me suspiciously.

"I'm not with the police."

He jangled his keys. He seemed nervous. That was good, right?

"A private eye?" he asked.

I shook my head. "Nope. Just a . . . a . . . friend of Jack's girlfriend." Referring to Tova as a friend felt odd. I'd spent a lot of time this past year disliking her.

"The lingerie model?" I could have sworn he snickered.

"Yes. She didn't know about Jack's life here."

He slung the backpack on his shoulder. "I told him to tell her, but he thought he knew better. Obviously not."

Obviously. "Did he tell anyone?"

He scoffed. "He was a coward." He crossed his arms and cocked a hip. "I need to get ready. It takes time to create fabulousness."

Whatever. But I wasn't giving up that easy. I had more questions, and he had plenty of time until the show started. "I talked to Danny Stone, the producer. He told me Jack took your spot on the show."

He shrugged. With an unconvincing laugh he said, "Jack wasn't even interested. Until that bitch Gwen showed up one night and threatened to destroy his reputation and practice. Suddenly, Jack had to be on the show. It wasn't his dream. It was my dream. My American dream," he wailed, arms flailing. The drama queen was on her throne.

It was hard not to get sidetracked by his performance. "Gwen, his office manager? She was here?"

"A couple of weeks ago. She's nosey, like you."

179

Why does everyone say that as if it's a bad thing?

"And they argued?" I asked. I knew Gwen was hiding something.

"She went all kinds of crazy on him. Said he'd lose his practice if people found out. Then she told him she'd kill him before she'd be made a fool of."

Had she? Was anger enough to give her the strength to strangle Dr. O'Doggle?

"Did you tell the police?" I asked.

"Girl, why would I talk to the po-po if I didn't have too? Okay, we're done here. I got to get ready. Bringing extravaganza and elegance to this dump isn't easy, you know. It takes work."

And with a snap, he was off. I followed him to the dressing room. It wasn't very large, but was filled to capacity. A couple of rusty clothes racks full of wardrobes pieces were shoved in the corner. All three dressing stations were barely large enough to store hairpieces and multiple trays of makeup. Each station had its own wall-mirror framed with dirty light bulbs. In the middle of the room stood Bea Haven, Goldie Fawn, and a drag queen I didn't recognize. All three were half-dressed. They were fighting.

"I said, your hair needs to be bigger." That

was Bea Haven. She didn't use as much padding as I'd previously thought. She was a naturally big girl. Tonight she was wrapped like a sausage in a black corset, boy-shorts, and go-go boots. She tried to grab the hair of the manly looking chick next to her.

"Leave my wig along. I don't style you, do I?" That dude's voice was too deep to pass for a woman — ever. He was half-dressed in black pantyhose and a padded girdle. His bra sported cone-shaped boobs no woman in her right mind would ever want. "You don't get it," he purred. "I'm the future of drag."

A futuristic drag queen?

David/Ladasha tossed her backpack onto the dressing table then strolled to the middle of the group, making it four drag queens. "Ladies, you need to get along."

When had she become the voice of reason?

I was having flashbacks to the Miss Texas competition. This was going to end poorly.

"No one said we had to like each other," Goldie said. She was dressed in a neon-blue cat suit, minus the cape.

"You don't like me?" Future Drag Queen turned pouty lips toward Goldie.

"You can't lip sync. And your makeup is hideous. First you "cook," then you blend. Figure it out," Goldie shouted.

She was right. Beauty Queen 101: to achieve the smooth flawless look, foundation needed to set for at least ten minutes to allow the makeup to melt into the skin.

Suddenly, Bea's spider eyelash dropped on the floor. "Oh!" she yelped. "Nobody move."

Goldie shook her head so hard her long black locks slapped her face. "She's not the only unpolished mess here." He pointed an accusing finger in David/Ladasha's direction.

David struck a runway pose, still dressed in street clothes. "I call it homeless chic."

Goldie spun around and cornered Future Queen. "You have no rhythm. What are you even doing here? You need to leave before you embarrass yourself even more."

She refused to be bullied. "You're so old you look like a man."

Everyone gasped. Including Bea, who was on her knees looking for her hairy eyelash.

"No you didn't. You did not just go there," Bea said.

Lord almighty. I was terrified, and they hadn't even noticed me yet.

"Take it back," Goldie ordered.

"No," Future Drag Queen said with a head snap, just in case the others hadn't caught her attitude. As if that was possible.

"Take it back, or I'll rip that cheap wig off your bald head," Goldie threatened in a low, menacing voice.

It was on.

I had a front row seat to a drag fight. Surprisingly, it wasn't much different than a behind-the-scenes catfight during a beauty pageant. Well, there was one difference. Here, the girly screaming came from grown men. Wigs, cutlets, padded underwear, and glitter flew everywhere. So did the curse words.

I hid in the background, out of the fray. A padded girdle flew past me and hit the mirror. It was then I noticed the photos of David and Jack. In one photo they were in drag. It was the same picture in the clipping we'd found. The other one was a candid shot of them at the gym. The photo had been torn, removing what looked like a third person. All that was left was an elbow. Who was it, and why had Ladasha ripped that person out of his life?

I pulled the photo off the mirror and slipped out the door to safety. Maybe I needed to check with Tova and find out if she'd ever heard of David.

# CHAPTER TWENTY-TWO

Tova's pad was on the way to Grey's place, which was handy since I was late for our dinner date. The night grew darker the closer I drove to Tova's house in the hills. I pulled into her drive and parked next to her yellow Hummer.

Funny thing about Tova's place. The house itself looked like a multi-million dollar home, spacious and extravagant, but she'd never landscaped the front yard, which kept it from looking completely finished.

The minute my boots hit the cement drive, I froze. See, not that long ago, I was in this exact spot for a totally different reason. I'd come to talk her out of her silly lawsuit about the fleas. She did finally drop it, but the whole experience tainted my already low opinion of Tova.

Who would have thought such a short time later I'd be here again, only this time to help her? I never thought my feelings would have shifted, but they had. At least enough to believe she wasn't capable of murder.

My pulse sped up with each step. I took a deep breath then knocked on the double-doors. The right door swung open. A feeling of déjà vu washed over me.

Tova's expression transformed from surprise, to confusion, and finally settled on excitement. Okay, that last part was not déjà vu. Last time I was here, she'd practically kicked me out on my butt.

"It's you." Her smile seemed a little too friendly, her eyes a little too unfocused. I quickly took in her oversized tunic and yoga pants. She looked disheveled.

"Can we talk?" I asked, then shuddered. I think that's what I'd said last time.

Barefoot, she stumbled backwards as she opened the door allowing me inside her sanctuary. "Come on in."

"Are you drunk?"

"Nope." She squinted at me, leaning on the door for support. "Are you?"

I leaned closer and sniffed. I didn't smell alcohol on her breath. She continued to stand there staring at me. Something wasn't right. She was barely upright.

I closed the door behind me. "Are you alone?"

She closed her eyes as she nodded. "Yessss."

I grabbed her by the elbow and started walking. This was my first time past the front door, and I had no idea where I was going. I guided her to what looked like a great room. A great, white room. Walls, carpet, furniture, even the art was void of color. Grey would say white is a color. Not me.

I eased Tova onto the couch. She flopped to her side.

"Are you on drugs?"

"I haven't been sleeping," she answered with her eyes closed. "Ambien doesn't work. I have something new. Something better. I want to tell you somethin'." She struggled to open her eyes. Whatever she was taking now was strong. Her mouth opened and closed, but nothing came out but a yawn.

"Do you have a blanket?"

"In my room," she managed to get out between a couple more yawns. Her breathing started to change into a steady cadence meant for deep sleep.

"I didn't want to sue you. That was all Stacie's idea." Her small voice floated throughout the room.

"Why would Stacie want you to sue me?"

Tova looked at me through silted eyes. "I don't remember now. You made me mad. You make me mad a lot. You think you're better than me, but you're not. I bought this house. I'm rich."

That sounded like the real Tova. "Where's Kiki?"

Tova's eyes closed. "My precious Kiki. She loves me. She won't leave me for wigs and formal wear."

I charged up the stairs looking for her dog and a blanket. I found both in Tova's bedroom. Kiki was curled up in her princess bed snoozing away, oblivious to her owner's state. When I yanked the blanket off the foot of the bed, I saw a bottle of pills on Tova's nightstand.

I walked over and picked them up. Valium. The prescription was in Stacie's name. I looked at the number on the label then quickly counted the remaining pills. Only three were gone.

I raced back to Tova and quickly covered her up.

"Did Stacie give you these?" I held out the pills.

Tova managed to open one eye halfway. "Isn't she the best assistant? Except for wanting to sue you. Why would she want to do that?"

I had no idea. "How many did you take?"

"Stacie said to take only one. They're very powerful."

Damn straight. "Where is she?"

Tova snuggled under the covers and closed her eyes. "Home."

I was losing her fast. "Tova, did Jack ever talk about a man named David?"

She shook her head no. "Yes."

"Which is it? Yes or no?"

"I'm sleepy. I want to go to bed now."

"In just a minute. Did Jack like Kiki?"

"He liked big dogs. He was always afraid he'd step on her."

"How often did Jack work out at the gym?"

Her brows furrowed as she tried to come up with an answer. "Every morning and every Saturday and Sunday night. He said it helped him unwind." She yawned again. "I'm going to sleep now."

Jack was a naughty boy. He wasn't at the gym Saturday and Sunday. Those were performance nights.

Leaving Tova in her current state seemed unsafe. Once I was sure snoring and drooling was all the reaction she'd experience for the night, I pocketed the pills and headed for Grey's. I couldn't take the chance Tova would wake up and down more pills.

When I got to Grey's and explained what happened, he called in a favor and asked a local doctor to check on Sleeping Beauty. After all was said and done, our fancy dinner at the restaurant ended up being a meal that neither of us enjoyed.

We agreed to take a drive north past Newport Beach, feeling subdued in our glamorous outfits — Grey in his Tom Ford suit and me in a new Carolina Herrera dress and Stuart Weitzman ankle-strap shoes.

The stars were bright, the moon full. But the tension between us shadowed everything.

On our way home, Grey's Mercedes floated along south on highway one, taking the corners effortlessly. I cracked the window so I could smell the ocean and hear the waves. The last hour of silence had worn me down.

"What are you thinking?" I asked, looking out the window at the ocean.

"You won't like it."

"I don't like the silence either," I muttered.

"I understood why you felt the need to help Darby. But Tova? That I don't get." His voice was tight.

I sighed. "What does it feel like when you capture a bad guy?"

"Now you're changing the subject."

I shook my head. "I'm not. Just answer the question."

When he didn't respond, I worried he was finished talking to me. I couldn't blame him.

"I've righted a wrong," he finally said.

I turned in my seat and stared at him. "Do you get an adrenaline rush? Does your heart race? Do you feel alive? Do you feel like you're contributing to the greater good?"

He glanced at me. "Are you telling me that is how you feel?"

I honestly thought about it, wanting to be truthful, but wanting him to understand. "Not exactly, but on some level. It's an adventure. And I'm good at it."

"You're good at sticking your nose in other people's business —"

We both heard it at the same time. A blaring horn in the distance. Grey slowed down. What seemed like a hundred yards of skid marks stained the road before us. Grey followed them and pulled over. A white Lexus sedan had driven off the side of the road and down an embankment.

"Stay here." He jumped out to offer assistance.

Of course, I followed. The salty air mixed

with the smell of burnt rubber, turning my stomach.

Grey reached the car while I was still skittering downhill in four-inch heels. I could see there was someone inside, their head on the steering wheel.

"Call for help," Grey called out.

I trudged back up the hill, further ruining my shoes. I pulled my cell out of Grey's SUV and called 9-1-1. I spouted all the information I knew and ended the call.

"An ambulance is on the way," I called out. I lost my balance and slid down the hill, barely managing to keep upright. I tottered to Grey's side.

"Are they okay?" I asked.

The driver's door was open. He crouched next to a woman, assessing her injuries. Under the glow of her car's interior light I realized she looked familiar.

I gasped recognizing the redhead. "Gwen?"

She rolled her head, looking in my direction. "He tried to kill me," she whispered.

"Who?" Grey asked.

She blinked a few times, trying to focus on our faces.

"It's going to be okay. Hang in there. Help is on the way," Grey's deep voice seemed to sooth her.

He stood, stepping back out of her earshot. "I've got a first aid kit. Keep her calm."

The night air chilled my bare arms. I rubbed them in an attempt to keep warm. "Can you grab a blanket, too?"

He charged back to his car while I returned to our injured murder suspect.

I bent next to her. "You said someone tried to kill you. Who?"

She looked confused. "I told him not to do it. But he wouldn't listen to me."

I guessed she was talking about Dr. O'Doggle. "Did you send his patients to another doctor?"

"We were going to lose everything. Appearance matters in our world. We were going to be a joke. No one wants a facelift by a drag queen." She raised her hand to her head. When she pulled it back, it was covered in blood. "Am I going to die?"

"I think you'll be okay." Grey was back with a towel and a plaid flannel blanket. I covered Gwen with the blanket. He held out the towel to her. "Hold this against your head. You're going to have a nasty headache."

"I already do," she mumbled.

Faint sirens in the distance slowly grew louder. I tried to reassure her. "You'll be out of here in no time."

"I didn't kill him," she said.

That's what they all say. "We'll talk later," I said.

A police cruiser and an ambulance pulled up. We stepped away and let the paramedics do their work. It sounded like Grey was right, and Gwen was going to be okay.

Once we were back in the Mercedes and headed toward home, Grey released the emotions building since before dinner. It was about to get ugly.

"That is why I want you to back off this case," he practically shouted. The muscles in his neck pushed against his white collar.

"You can't be serious."

"Of course, I am. That could have been you. We don't know who's stalking her. That person may want you out of the picture, too."

"She has a head injury. She could have been talking about some maniac with road rage."

Deep down, neither of us believed it.

"I'll talk to Malone first thing tomorrow," I promised.

It was one promise I wasn't looking forward to keeping.

# CHAPTER TWENTY-THREE

Facing Grey had been much easier than facing Malone. Especially when he came looking for me and not the other way around. My only saving grace was that Betty was with me. She was in her usual silk pajamas, pearls, and white sneakers. Today her eyebrows were jungle red. Perfect for keeping Malone off balance.

The minute Betty noticed the good-looking detective, she sauntered up next to him and wiggled her lipstick eyebrows. "Hey there, hot stuff, you're an attractive man. Do you have a girlfriend?"

Malone shoved his hands into the pockets of his black leather jacket. "Melinda?"

I bit my lip, holding back my laughter. It wasn't every day anyone made Judd Malone uncomfortable. "This is Betty. She's helping me part-time. Betty, this is Detective Malone."

"A detective, uh? Cookie's taken." She

nudged him with her hip. "But I've got something for you to investigate."

Malone looked like he was choking. He looked at Betty and then at me. "Can we step into your office?"

The moment of truth. I'd feel more confident if I'd worn my typical attire, but today I'd semi-dressed up. I'd traded my boots for flats, and instead of jeans and T-shirt, I'd pulled on jeans and sweater. Not a huge difference, but it was easier to be cheeky when dressed in a tee with "I'd rather be with my dog" splashed cross the front than in a Kate Spade beach sweater.

"Betty, can you hold down the fort for a few minutes?"

"Sure. But don't get any ideas, handsome. She's engaged to an art dealer. And he's a hottie. Hot, hot, hot."

"He knows all about Grey. If you need anything, we'll just be in my office." I motioned for Malone to follow me.

She fanned herself as Malone passed by. "Sure thing, Cookie."

I'd made fun of the detective's miniature office, but to be honest, mine was only a wee bit larger. We each took a chair. Since we were on my turf, I got the one behind the desk.

"I talked to your friend, Gwen, last night," he said.

"How is she? Is she still in the hospital?"

"She spent a few hours in the ER. She'll be okay."

"Did she tell you about Jack and the drag queens?"

"Yes."

"Did she tell you she was sending his patients to other doctors?"

"Yes."

"Did she tell you about the reality show?"

"Yes."

I settled back, basking in the power of the knowledge I held for the moment. A brief moment, but it was real, and I wanted to enjoy it. I admit, I could have found a way to tell Malone all of this myself, but what if I'd been wrong? I guess that was better than withholding information. It was time to come clean with everything I knew. "I bet she didn't tell you Jack stole that part from David, aka Ladasha."

He dragged his hand through his hair. "Why can't you obey orders? I've made myself very clear."

"You have. For the most part. I don't do so well when people tell me what to do. I know, you're different. You have the law on your side. Trust me, I know."

"I wouldn't know it by the way you blatantly disregard instructions to stay out of my investigation."

I leaned forward. "If it wasn't for me, you might not have known about Jack's secret life as Jackie O."

"Do I need to threaten you with jail in order to keep your nose out of police business?"

"Why can't you just admit it? I was helpful to you. Did you talk to the ladies at the Kitty Kat Club?"

Was it my imagination, or did he blush? "Yes."

"That reminds me. Did I tell you that Goldie Fawn bought a green lead from me?"

"No. which one was he?"

"She was Cat Woman. Her real name is Kevin. Paid with a credit card. Also, I was talking to Dr. Stolzman, and he made an interesting point. He said whoever killed Jack had to be a man."

Malone's intense eyes narrowed. "How'd he come up with that conclusion?"

"He said it takes a lot of strength and stamina to perform the types of surgeries they do. Jack worked out every morning. Dedicated. If he was as strong as Dr. Stolzman suggested, how could someone get the drop on him, strangle him, and him not fight back? Doesn't that rule out all women? Did you find fingerprints? If not, does that mean the killer wore some type of glove? Ladasha wears gloves as part of her costume."

Super Cop didn't say a word. He stared at me with an unreadable face.

"Blink once if I'm on the right track."

"You've been very helpful. But it's time for you to step back."

"You know I'm not a Tova fan. But I don't think she did it. I saw her last night, she was a mess." I left out the part about her taking a prescription drug that didn't belong to her. "She's so upset about the whole situation she's not sleeping. She's not strong enough to carry a dog that weighs more than five pounds. There's no way she could have choked her boyfriend."

He rubbed his face. "I'll tell you this much. Jack O'Doggle was killed with his own leash. We looked though his house in Balboa Island and the leash was gone. According to Tova and her assistant, the leash was kept at his place. The only prints on the leash belonged to O'Doggle."

So whoever killed him had probably worn gloves. "That would make sense. Except according to Stacie, Jack hated dogs. She said that was one of the reasons he hadn't

198

proposed to Tova. Although when I asked Tova, she said Jack liked big dogs because he was afraid of stepping on Kiki. That sounds possible. Or it could all be a lie. One thing we do know — he wasn't ready to reveal his drag queen hobby to the world. Until recently. Then he went about it under-handedly."

"Now what are you talking about?"

"Originally, Ladasha was cast for the reality show. Then one night, Gwen followed Jack to the club and discovered his secret. She threatened to ruin his practice."

"You have that part wrong. Gwen admitted she threatened to blackmail him. She wanted the money in case the practice folded once word got out about Dr. O'Doggle's moonlighting."

Gwen was a shrewd gal. "I guess Jack decided that he had no choice but to tell the world on his own terms. That's when he auditioned for the show. Too bad the producer loved Jackie O so much that he replaced Ladasha with him."

"Ladasha told you all of this?"

"With some details from Danny Stone."

"Another drag queen?"

"No. The producer of the reality show. He gave me his card. I thought you'd like to talk to him." I stood up and dug Danny's business card from the bottom of my purse. "He also said Ladasha threatened to make Jack pay." I handed him the contact information. "Drag queens wear gloves. Elbow-length gloves. And Gwen had said, 'He tried to kill me.' "

"Stop talking." He waved the card. "How did you find out about Danny Stone?"

"The drag queens. I thought you talked to them."

"They failed to mention that part. By the way, where'd you find Betty?"

I smiled. "She found me. If you want me to set you up . . ."

He stood, ending the conversation.

"I'll take that as a 'No,' " I said.

On his way out the door he said, "Keep your nose clean."

"Of course."

# CHAPTER TWENTY-FOUR

During the afternoon, a steady flow of customers filed through the store. Betty worked the crowd like a pro. The supply of paw-lish had evaporated since her arrival. I made a mental note to request twice the amount of stock when I reordered.

Betty finished ringing up a special order of Pooch Smooch Cologne for Luis Cruz and his long-haired dachshund, Barney.

Betty studied Barney with skepticism. "Why is he a dressed like a wiener?"

Luis enjoyed dressing his pup in a wide array of Halloween costumes, regardless the time of year. Today he was a hot dog. Last week, the tooth fairy.

Luis ran his hand through his thick black hair, looking more than a tad embarrassed. "He's a little bloated today. It's the only costume that fit."

"You should put him on a diet. We have special dog food. Dr. Darling highly recommends it." She pointed at the sad-faced hot dog drooling on the floor. "He should try it."

I walked around the counter. "I think you look pretty good, Barney."

Hearing his name, Barney barked and wagged his long body. I bent down and slipped him a treat, away from Betty's watchful eye.

"Thanks, Mel. Doc said his goiter's gone."

"That's good news. Betty's actually on to something. The next time you see Dr. Darling, ask about putting Barney on a special diet. You don't have to buy it here, but promise you'll ask about the possibility."

Luis nodded. "Sure, if you think so." He took his cologne and left.

"Cookie, we're never gonna make any money if you tell people they can shop somewhere else. I thought you were smart?"

I patted Betty's thin arm. "How about you stop worrying about how much money I'm making?"

"It's kinda hard when you keep locking the customers out. Or sending them to another store. I want my paycheck."

I chuckled. "Sugar, you have a job, and a paycheck, for as long as you want one. Got it?"

She eyed me. "What about a raise?"

I loved her pluck. "If you can sell something other than nail polish, we'll talk."

Betty grabbed one of the extra cans of cologne. "Does he really use this?" She spritzed her arm. Immediately, the scent of coconut filled the shop. "That's nasty. No one's going to buy this stuff."

"Luis did. He requested it."

"Yeah, well, he dresses his wiener dog like a trick-or-treater. Now he's forcing him to smell like a Piña Colada. I don't think he's a reliable market." She dropped the can on the counter by the register. "You should return this and get our money back."

The phone rang, ending the day's business management lesson by Professor Foxx.

"Bow Wow Boutique, how can I help you?" She listened for a second, then held out the receiver. "It's for you."

"Thanks." I took the cordless from her. "This is Melinda."

"It's Dr. Stolzman. I wanted to thank you for helping Gwen last night."

"Of course. How is she?"

"She's got a good-size knot on her head and a few stitches, but she'll be okay in a couple of days."

I noticed Betty eavesdropping. I meandered toward the dog bowls, in the opposite direction. "That's good to hear."

"She's adamant someone ran her off the road."

Not just anyone. A "he" someone. My money was on David, aka Ladasha. "That's what she said last night. Did she get a good look at him?"

"No. It was dark and the other driver had his high beams on. She thought she saw a yellow Hummer."

My heart dropped. Tova. But Tova was in no condition to drive last night. Was it a co-incidence? Was someone setting her up to take the fall? "Is she sure about the Hummer?" I asked.

"That's what she told the police. Look, I have a facelift scheduled in twenty minutes so I have to make this quick. This morning at the gym, I talked to a guy on the staff who hinted he knows who killed Jack."

"Who?"

"He wouldn't tell me. Said his boss would fire him for ratting out a client."

I shook my head stunned at the absurdity of his comment. "That's ridiculous. He needs to talk to the police."

"I agree. Would you go to the gym and see if you can convince him to talk to that detective? Maybe a pretty face will persuade him."

I doubted that, but I'd give it a shot. "I

can try. What's this guy's name?"

"Tony. He runs the juice bar. Thanks. Let me know what happens."

I handed the phone back to Betty.

"You're leaving again." She stated the obvious.

"I'll be back in an hour." I grabbed my cell and purse.

"Sure, sure. That's what you always say."

She had a point. Before I walked out the door, I double checked I still had the torn photo of Jack and Ladasha at the gym. Maybe someone there could tell me who the missing third person was.

Within thirty minutes, I breezed through the doors of Jim Chow's gym. It smelled like a bleached-out locker room. The echo of metal slapping metal filled the entryway.

I roamed around until I found the juice bar in the weight room. There were a dozen men pumping iron, grunting out their number of reps. I headed for the blond-haired hulk who stood behind a wooden counter, dumping scoops of powder in a blender.

"Are you Tony?" I asked.

His dark shark eyes looked me up and down. "You bet. What can I do you for, gorgeous?"

Eck. I automatically stepped back, widening my personal space. Now I understood why the doc wanted me to come instead of him. "I'm a friend of Dr. Stolzman's."

"You don't need any nips or tucks, sweetheart. You need some help with that great body? You come see me. I'll train you personally."

I ignored the muscles rippling under his T-shirt and pulled out the photograph. I gingerly pushed it across the counter. "Do you know these guys?"

"Sure. That's Dr. O'Doggle and David Harncik. David's a funny guy. Doesn't like to sweat. He has a thing for my creatine shakes. Pull up a stool. I'll make you one," he added with a wink.

I held up my hand. "No thanks, I just ate." The lie flowed off my tongue too easily. Anything to keep him at arm's length. "Did they work out together?"

"Sometimes."

"Did they work out last Thursday morning?"

"What's the deal with all the questions? Are you a cop?" His oily charm evaporated into mistrust.

"No. But if you have information about Dr. O'Doggle's death, you need to tell the police."

"I don't know who killed the doc." He pulled out a damp towel and wiped down the bar.

"But you know something."

He looked around as if he expected someone to be listening to our conversation. Trust me, no one was paying any attention to us, but that didn't seem to matter to him. He acted spooked. "Who told you that?"

"Does it matter? Someone's missing from the photo. Do you know who?"

"Sure. The three of them were working out, like always, then the chick goes crazy. Yelling about how family is supposed to stick together and calling one of them a traitor and a backstabber and how he thought he was better than them and needed to pay for it. She lost her mind."

"The chick?"

"I wouldn't mess with her. She's got major anger management issues. She threatens to sue the gym at least once a month for something. Since the doc died, she and the guy haven't been back."

"They were family? Is the 'sister' a tall redhead? Do you know her name?"

"Stacie." My legs about gave out on me. I was speechless, so he kept talking. "Average height, really athletic. Light brown hair. I think she works with the doc's girlfriend."

"Whose sister is she?"

His beefy index finger covered Ladasha's face on the photo. "His. I snapped this picture with David's cell phone right over there. Those were happier times. Before psycho threatened to sue the doc for stealing her brother's part in some movie or TV show."

I ran my fingers through my hair, pulling it away from my face. "When was this?"

He shrugged. At least I think he did. It was hard to tell since he didn't have much of a neck. Just a lot of muscles. "I don't know, a few weeks ago, maybe."

"Then what happened?" I asked.

"Out of the blue, they all show up again like they're back to being pals, but you could tell they were just pretending. That's when the doc and David argued again. She's the one who calmed them down. Then she came over here and bought a round of post-workout shakes for her and David. She brought some kind of special protein powder to use in the doc's. I made his shake with that."

Oh my gosh. Had Stacie drugged Jack with the same pills she'd given Tova? That's how she was able to strangle him without him overpowering her?

It was time to call in the big guns. Tony

had some explaining to do, and I didn't want to be around when he did. "Can I use your phone?"

"Sure."

With shaky hands, I pulled up my contact list on my cell and found the number I needed. I grabbed the phone from Tony and punched it in.

Pick up, pick up.

"Malone." His commanding tone was actually welcome, for a change.

"Thank God you're there. Please don't lecture, just listen. I didn't tell you that when I was with Tova last night, she'd taken some Valium left there by her assistant, Stacie."

"What —"

I squeezed the phone tighter. "Listen now. Yell later. Ladasha is Stacie's brother. They work out at the same gym as Jack. I think Stacie drugged Jack, lured him to the sidewalk in front of Bow Wow, and killed him."

"Where are you?" He asked in his no nonsense cop tone.

"I'm at the Jim Chow's Fitness for Life gym in Newport Beach. I have someone who needs to talk to you. Hear him out. If he hangs up, call him back."

I thrust the phone at Tony. "You talk to

Detective Malone right now. Tell him everything you told me, or he'll drive over here and toss you in jail."

"I'll lose my job," he argued in a hushed voice.

I raised an eyebrow and punctuated each word with determination. "You'll lose more than that in county lockup. You know what I mean?"

He grimaced.

I shook the phone, urging him to take it. "Do it."

He cracked his knuckles, then took the receiver from me. "Yo."

I left him to tell his story to Malone, my good deed done for the day. My mind raced as I added all the details. Stacie and David were siblings. I didn't see that one. She was overprotective, and it sounded like she had some serious anger issues. And, she liked to sue people, which explained why she urged Tova to sue me about the fleas. Well, not completely.

Tova said she'd lost her bracelet the night of my party. Stacie could have found it and planted it under Jack's body to implicate Tova. What a crazy mess.

I walked through the parking lot to my Jeep and skittered to a stop.

I lost my breath for a second, blinking and

praying I wasn't seeing what was in front of me. Someone had vandalized my beautiful Jeep. The windows were smashed, the doors bashed in, and all four tires slashed.

Hells bells.

# CHAPTER TWENTY-FIVE

I was honked off. I couldn't believe someone had taken a bat to my Jeep like a scorned lover. I called Darby for a ride, but she was in the middle of a photo shoot for the calendar. Grey and I were still fighting, and the last thing I wanted right now was a well-meaning speech. There was Caro, but as we all know, my cousin and I weren't speaking.

So I called Betty. She was thrilled to give me a ride.

While I waited, I snapped pictures with my cell and emailed them to myself. I'd have to get a rental while my car was in the shop.

It hadn't occurred to me until now that I didn't know what type of car Betty drove, so when a Mini Cooper zipped into the parking lot, I had no idea it was my ride until the window lowered and an older female voice shouted, "Let's go, Cookie, I don't have all day."

Great. Did I mention I hate small cars?

I barely had time to buckle my seatbelt when Betty peeled out of the parking lot, jumping the curb. Holy crapola.

"Sidewalks are for pedestrians only." I should have pressed Betty to let me drive her car.

She was hunched over the steering wheel in concentration. "I missed them by a mile."

Her Mini Cooper raced down the road, blowing through a major intersection, almost sideswiping a bus. I gasped. We were going to die. I should have called Grey.

"Are you trying to kill us?" I cried out.

"I'm a great driver." She pressed the gas.

"You are a horrible driver."

We zigzagged down PCH toward Laguna Beach, straddling the painted white line more often than not. I grabbed the Oh-Crap handle above my head.

"What's the big emergency?" I asked.

Betty zoomed up to a red light and slammed on the brakes, throwing us forward. "I had to shoo away some customers to come get you. I told them to come back in an hour."

The light turned green. Betty hit the gas, and the tires squealed. We rolled into town in record time. I'd finally caught my breath as we turned onto Forest heading toward the boutique. I recognized the yellow Hummer in front of us.

I could tell from the side mirror, Tova wasn't the driver.

"Do you mind if we make a quick stop before we go back to the shop?"

"You're the boss. Where to?"

"Follow that Hummer."

Betty rubbed her hands together and let out a Texas-sized holler. "Hot Damn. I love a good car chase."

What have I done?

I should have known Stacie would head straight for the Kitty Kat club. Race Car Betty sped around back so Psycho Stacie wouldn't see us. By the time we circled, the Hummer was in the parking lot with a handful of other vehicles.

"This place is a dump," Betty said.

"It's much more exotic at night."

"Sure. You can't see it. What are we doing here, anyway?"

"That was Tova's assistant. I think she's the one who vandalized my Jeep." Among many other despicable acts. "Pull up next to the Hummer. I want to look inside."

Betty pulled up. I jumped out and peeked through the window. Sure enough, on the floorboard was a baseball bat. A Louisville

Slugger.

I hopped back into the Mini Cooper. "Let's get out of here."

Betty looked crestfallen. "Aren't we gonna go inside and confront her? Take her down?"

"She brutalized my Jeep, killed Dr. O'Doggle, and probably ran Gwen off the road. Even I don't want to take her on." Especially with Betty as a sidekick.

"Wow." Betty revved the engine. "I didn't peg you for a party pooper."

Neither did I.

# CHAPTER TWENTY-SIX

The entire trip back to Bow Wow, Betty continued to express her disappointment about not going inside the club. I was too busy praying for our safe arrival that I missed most of it.

When we got back to the boutique, I called Malone and filled him in about the Jeep beating and the bat in Tova's Hummer. I told him I was worried about Tova, too. He promised to send a couple of uniformed officers to her place to check on her.

Then he left me speechless, which doesn't happen often. Me being speechless, that is. He thanked me for not doing anything stupid.

It was official. We'd turned a corner in our relationship.

I sent a disappointed Betty home while I closed up. She was still running high on adrenaline, spouting off her allegiance to justice and revenge. Frankly, I didn't think her daughter was going to let her continue working for me. Not that I could blame her.

At some point, it dawned on me that Betty was a glimpse into my future. At moments, I found myself amused and other times sympathetic and grateful to those who loved me. But I had one heck of a future ahead of me.

Speaking of the latter, the last call I made was to Grey. He didn't answer, so I left him a message asking if he'd pick me up at the shop. I only said I'd had some car trouble.

I was in my office, shutting down the computer when the front door chimed. Betty must have forgotten to lock it behind her. More likely, she was back with a new argument as to why we should go spy on Stacie.

I grabbed my purse and ambled out front. "What'd you forget?"

"Not a thing," Stacie said sarcastically.

Obviously not. She had a gun. And it was pointed at Betty's side.

I felt sick. I held up my hands and, in the process, dropped my purse on the floor. "Betty doesn't know anything."

Stacie nodded her head in mock sadness. "Yes, she does."

"Sorry, Cookie. I got a little excited when I saw her heading your way. I may have let it slip about her killing the doc."

I sighed. Trying to control Betty was like trying to tame a hurricane.

"You don't want to do this, Stacie. I've talked to Malone. He knows everything."

She shoved Betty toward me. "You two are so annoying. Can't you take a hint?" Stacie's angry green eyes glared at me. She leveled her gun at my heart.

I stepped back, straight into the damn Christmas tree Betty'd set up in the middle of the store. "Obviously. I figured out you killed Jack."

"You're a naughty girl," Betty said. She wagged her finger at Stacie. "That very attractive detective is going to throw you in jail." I yanked Betty to my side and backed up another inch or two, trying to put space between us and the gun. The tree blocked my way.

Stacie whipped her gun in Betty's direction. "Shut up. I'm done listening to your smart mouth." With a few steps, she closed the gap between us, kicking my purse out of reach.

Betty hissed. "I knew you were bad news. You can't bamboozle me, Tootsie. I've got your number."

I squeezed Betty's arm, willing her to stop antagonizing the lady with the deadly weapon. I couldn't think with them snapping at each other.

My cell was in my purse, and Darby was still in the middle of a photo shoot. Grey was MIA and Malone was . . . doing police stuff just blocks away. Where were the cops when you needed them?

Hells bells, if Stacie didn't kill me, Betty's daughter would.

"You should let Betty go. She can't hurt you," I said, stalling as I racked my brain for a way out alive.

"No." the gun waved between Betty and me. I noticed the rash still on Stacie's hands. Of course. The rash was the final piece. "I'm going to shoot both of you. I just have to choose which one is first."

Rock, paper, scissors didn't work out so well for me. I pressed my lips together, keeping my smart-aleck comments to myself.

A prickly pine branch pressed against my back. I shuffled Betty over a few inches so I could find some relief from the blasted tree.

There was nothing I could use to defend us other than a handful of shampoo and conditioner, a can of dog perfume, and . . .

The dog cologne. That was it.

"Betty, don't worry." I continued to shuffle us backwards. "She hates me more. I have proof she killed Jack and that she was the one who ran Gwen off the road." Of course I was lying. I had nothing.

"I didn't leave behind any proof," Stacie snarled.

"Because of the gloves? That's how you got the rash. It's not poison ivy, is it? Did you know you were allergic to latex before you stole the box of gloves from Dr. O's office?"

Her eyes widened in surprise. "How'd you know?"

I'd guessed about stealing the box from Jack's office. She could have just as easily bought a box from the local drug store. But Stacie seemed to like living life on the edge. "I interviewed a potential employee who was allergic to latex. She told me all about her symptoms. Even brought me a box of latex-free gloves to keep at the boutique."

Betty snorted. "Are you talking about that nut job, Vera? You almost gave her my job?"

"You could have taken her in a fair fight." I looked at Betty and shifted my eyes toward the Christmas tree, trying to telegraph what I was thinking. I wasn't sure Betty was paying any attention.

"What I don't get is how you got Jack out front," I said to Stacie. I continued to stall as I attempted to maneuver us into the perfect position.

Stacie stepped closer. "Stop moving."

Our feet froze in place. I had to keep her talking.

"How'd you do it, Stacie? Did you drive him here?"

"It was easy. He was so desperate to make up with my brother. He did whatever I said. I told him you agreed to meet him here first thing in the morning to turn over those stupid dog booties. You played into my hand perfectly when you refused to give Tova his gift. He got in my car without a complaint."

"You drugged his shake so that by the time you got here —"

"He was almost asleep. He told David and me all about his great plan to be a famous drag queen plastic surgeon. I just helped him reach his celebrity status quicker. Don't you get it? Dr. O'Doggle was strangled with his girlfriend's dog leash in front of Bow Wow Dog Boutique?"

Every time we stepped back, Stacie unconsciously stepped forward. I just needed Stacie to take one more step closer. "Is that why you planted Tova's bracelet on him?"

Her lips curved into a nasty smile. "That was my excuse to see him at the gym. My peace offering. I told him the clasp was broke and Tova had lost it. He must have put it in his pocket."

"What were you looking for when you and Tova were here?"

"That was all for Tova's benefit. She was still looking for her bracelet. And being the amazing assistant, I was helping her." Stacie lifted her chin and stared me in the eye. "I'm finished talking."

I guess she'd made up her mind who she was shooting first.

Betty narrowed her lipstick eyebrows and pursed her lips. "I'm not going down without a fight." She shuffled toward Stacie.

Stacie turned away from me. "Hold it right there, Grandma."

"I'm not your grandma," Betty shouted.

I lunged for the Christmas tree and pushed it onto Stacie. She screamed, stumbling backwards and dropping the gun.

"Run," I yelled to Betty.

I grabbed the can of Pooch Smooch Cologne from the counter and sprayed it in Stacie's face. Just for good measure.

Betty wasn't about to be left out of the action. She hopped up on Stacie's back and wrapped her tiny legs around her waist. "You're going down, Cupcake," she hollered.

Stacie tugged on Betty's arms. "You're choking me," she gagged. "Let go."

I grabbed the gun. "Betty, let her go."

"No way."

Stacie spun in circles, trying to toss Betty. "Get off, get off." Stacie reached behind her head, whacking at Betty. It was like a scene from a World Wrestling Federation match.

"Betty, stop! I've got the gun."

Betty loosened her hold and slid down Stacie's back. Her sneakers hit the floor with a firm thud. "Why didn't you say so?"

I didn't take my eyes off Stacie. "Betty, call the police and ask them to send Detective Malone."

"Oh, goodie. I like that yummy detective. Let me freshen up, first."

"I can't believe I got taken down by Nancy Drew and her grandma," Stacie sneered.

I smiled. I loved Nancy Drew. "Consider the Case of the Murdered Plastic Surgeon solved," I said.

"I like the Secret Life of a Drag Queen," Betty argued.

Out of nowhere, Malone burst through front door. "Police."

"How'd you know?" I asked, relieved to see him.

"Tova's yellow Hummer's parked in front of the shop. I was looking for it. You can put the gun down."

I lowered the weapon. Malone cuffed Stacie and told her to sit on the floor.

I was next to receive his attention. He held out his hand. I happily gave him the gun and managed a shaky smile. "Sorry I didn't call. As you can see, I was detained."

"Are you okay?"

I nodded. "I can explain everything."

He shook his head. "No, you can't."

Malone called for backup, and soon the boutique was once again bustling with police. I asked if I could go next door and fill Darby in, knowing she'd be worried. He agreed, but I was to come back so someone could take my statement. He even offered to give me a ride home.

I politely declined. I'd rather take my chances with Grey, who I hadn't called yet. Even Betty seemed like a safer choice than a cross cop.

Betty was in her element, being the center of attention in a room full of attractive men. As I was heading toward the door, I saw her lift her silk pajama pant, exposing her leg to a handsome young police officer.

"Darn." She batted her eyes at him. "I've got a run in my pantyhose."

# CHAPTER TWENTY-SEVEN

After Stacie was dragged off in handcuffs and tossed behind bars, Malone warned us that we might be called to testify at the trial. I wasn't so keen on the idea, but Betty, on the other hand, began planning what outfit she should wear.

Betty finally talked Darby and me into taking her to the Kitty Kat Club. It was a mistake. She dressed in her version of a drag outfit and managed to talk her way on stage. Naturally, she was a hit. She wants to go back.

Ladasha, Bea Haven, and Goldie Fawn dedicated a performance to their drag sister, Jackie O. There were tears, insults (aka "shade"), and a plethora of air kisses. I think Jack would have been very proud.

Once Gwen made a full recovery, she pressed assault charges against Stacie. Stacie threatened to sue everyone including the police.

As for Tova, she and Kiki wrapped up their photo shoot with Darby then left on a vacation to an undisclosed location. I couldn't blame her, really. It seemed everyone in her inner circle had lied to her, and she needed to find her bearings. I wouldn't call us friends, but we were no longer enemies. I was okay with that.

As for me, I was driving around town in a rented Lexus. I hated it. Grey and I stopped squabbling and made up. I agreed to make more of an effort to steer clear of dangerous situations. Grey agreed to trust me to make smart choices.

For now, I had everything I wanted, including Grandma Tillie's brooch.

Missy and I were at Paw Prints, taking our turn at modeling. Darby decided to use us for the month of December. She even talked Grey into playing Santa Claus with a white beard and a pillow for a belly. I pinned the brooch — the ghastly heirloom I loved so dearly — to my elf costume. Bless her heart, Darby didn't protest. She just let me flaunt the pin in each shot. I promised we'd take a few without my brooch at the end.

"Mel, straighten Missy's crown," Darby instructed from behind the camera.

Jingle Bell Rock played in the background,

setting the mood. The Brenda Lee version. I preferred traditional Christmas music.

As I reached over and adjusted the tiara, my hair brushed Missy's face. She sneezed, shooting dog slobber everywhere.

"Where's that rag?" I asked. One thing about owning a bulldog, you're always cleaning up drool.

Grey pulled the missing rag from his pocket. I wiped down my arm and then the folds of Missy's face. I planted a kiss on Santa's nose as I handed him the rag back. I heard the camera's fast successions of clicks capturing the moment.

"Mel, put her on Grey's lap so I have her profile. Then Grey, you lean down as if Missy's telling you what she wants for Christmas. Mel, I want you to hold the mistletoe above Santa's head. Then look at the camera and wink."

Lordy, she was bossy.

"Move your hair back, it's covering the brooch."

"Wouldn't want that," Grey muttered. "Can't we take one photo without that thing?"

"Stop talking and smile," Darby ordered.

After a few more poses, we were done. "That's a wrap," Darby called out.

"Will you take one of me on Santa's lap?" I asked.

"Only if you take off the ugly brooch," Grey insisted.

I looked at Darby, who wasn't bothering to hide her laughter. She held out her hand. I hadn't let the brooch out of my sight since I'd retrieved it from Caro's car. I'd been carrying it around in its box, tucked away in my purse for safe keeping.

Reluctantly, I handed the pin to Darby. She made a big show of nestling the brooch in the box. She walked it over to the counter and just left it there. Seriously, she left my pin unattended.

Grey pulled me into his lap and nuzzled my neck. I tried to get into the mood, but I kept thinking about the brooch, which was no longer in my line of sight.

Grey tightened his grip. "Relax. It's not as if she's going to walk in here and take it. She doesn't even know you have it," he whispered in my ear.

Yes, she did. She knew me backwards and forwards. Inside and out. That brooch meant just as much to her as it did to me.

Darby kept snapping photos, and I willed myself to relax. Grey whispered his idea for how we should spend the rest of the evening.

My heart skipped a beat, and I felt my face blush.

Snap.

"That's the one," Darby said.

I hopped off Grey's lap. "I'm going to change. Stay here and keep an eye on my pin. I'll be right back."

I headed toward the changing room. I'd just slipped off my skirt when I heard her.

Damn.

I rushed out of the dressing room in my pantyhose and Elf shirt with white fur collar. Grey and Darby were distracted, their backs turned as they packed up her photo equipment.

"Put that back, Carolina Lamont," I yelled.

Caro whipped around. She smiled wickedly. "Come make me, Melinda Langston."

Those were fighting words. I took off like a shot. So did Caro. She charged out the front door. I was right on her heels, until Grey, still dressed as Santa, grabbed me around the waist and stopped me.

"You can't go running through downtown in your underwear."

I didn't care what I was or was not wearing. My brooch-stealing cousin was getting away.

"The hell I can't. She's got my brooch."

Grey shook his head and sighed, tightening his hold on me. "What goes around comes around, Mel. Tonight, the brooch is Caro's."

We'd see about that.

# RECIPE

### YAPPY HOUR PUPCAKES
(Served by Mel & Darby at their Yappy Hour event)

You'll need the following ingredients:

2 carrots, grated
2 ripe bananas, mashed
1 egg
3 cups water
1/2 teaspoon vanilla
2 tablespoons honey
4 cups flour
1 teaspoon baking powder
1 teaspoon nutmeg
1 teaspoon cinnamon

Preheat your oven to 350 degrees.

Line a cupcake tin with festive dog-themed cupcakes papers.

Blend water, carrots, egg, vanilla and honey in a big bowl. Then add the mashed bananas.

In another bowl, blend the flour, baking powder, nutmeg and cinnamon.

Add the flour mix to the first (carrot/egg) mixture and blend them together thoroughly.

Spoon the mixture into the cupcake papers.

Bake the pupcakes for 30 minutes. Times can vary depending on your oven so it's a good idea to test the pupcakes by inserting a toothpick in the middle. If it comes out clean, your pupcakes are done.

Frosting is optional, but if you want to add frosting here's a quick idea.

2 tablespoons plain yogurt
2 tablespoons honey
1 package (6 oz.) cream cheese

Mix the ingredients together until smooth, frost the cooled pupcakes, and serve.

### CARO'S HOMEMADE KITTY COOKIES

This recipe uses shredded chicken (don't tell Walter) but you can use beef or fish, if your cat prefers it.

You'll need the following ingredients:

1-1/2 cups of cooked chicken, shredded into
   small pieces
1 cup of whole wheat flour
1/2 cup of chicken broth
1/3 cup of cornmeal
1 teaspoon of margarine, softened

Preheat your oven to 350 degrees

Mix the chicken, margarine, and chicken broth in a bowl. Then add the cornmeal and flour.

Knead the dough into a ball and roll it out to about 1/4 inch in thickness.

Cut into one inch pieces and place on an ungreased cookie sheet. Bake for 20 minutes and let cool.

This recipe makes 18-24 cookies.

Remember, these treats contain no preservatives and so unlike commercial treats, you need to make sure to store them with that in mind.

Caro recommends refrigerating unused portions and labeling them with the date they were made.

# ACKNOWLEDGEMENTS

We knew we were out of our league after a marathon night of *RuPaul's Drag Race*. Let's be honest here, what do two gals from Iowa know about drag queens? The Internet is an amazing tool, with a plethora of information at our fingertips, but every writer knows the best research is what you learn in person. We did our best to represent the drag queen community with humor and respect, and we hope that shows.

Jason W, thank you for explaining drag terminology, loaning us books we'd have never found on our own, and encouraging (okay, dragging,) us to visit Des Moines' very own drag show at The Garden. It was a night we'll never forget, and we have the photos to prove it. We hope we captured the fun we experienced that night.

To the ladies at The Garden who performed

the night of our visit, thank you for a fabulous show. We sang, cheered, danced and handed over a few dollar bills. You were the muse for our "ladies."

A big *Thank you* to our critique group, who were more than willing to brainstorm drag queen names, some of which will never be spoken again.

Karen M, thank you for sharing your zany Grandma Maxine stories. May your Maxine live forever in Betty.

Thank you to the amazing team at Bell Bridge Books, who continues to support and encourage us, even when we come up with crazy ideas like Pampered Pet Bingo. We love working with you!

As always, to our families, *Thank you* will never be enough. We love you.

And lastly, to our readers. You humble us with your enthusiasm for more Caro and Mel stories. It's because of you that we get to do what we love. Thank you. We love hearing from you and we love your pet stories. Keep them coming!

Mary Lee and Anita, aka Sparkle Abbey
www.SparkleAbbey.com

# ABOUT THE AUTHORS

**Sparkle Abbey** is the pseudonym of two mystery authors (Mary Lee Woods and Anita Carter). They are friends and neighbors as well as co-writers of the Pampered Pets Mystery Series. The pen name was created by combining the names of their rescue pets — Sparkle (Mary Lee's cat) and Abbey (Anita's dog). They reside in central Iowa, but if they could write anywhere, you would find them on the beach with their laptops and depending on the time of day, with either an iced tea or a margarita.

### Mary Lee
**Mary Lee Salsbury Woods** is the "Sparkle" half of Sparkle Abbey. She is past-president of Sisters in Crime — Iowa and a member of Mystery Writers of America, Romance Writers of America, Kiss of Death, the RWA Mystery Suspense chapter, Sisters

in Crime, and the SinC internet group Guppies.

Prior to publishing the Pampered Pet Mystery series with Bell Bridge Books, Mary Lee won first place in the Daphne du Maurier contest, sponsored by the Kiss of Death chapter of RWA, and was a finalist in Murder in the Grove's mystery contest, as well as Killer Nashville's Claymore Dagger contest.

Mary Lee is an avid reader and supporter of public libraries. She lives in Central Iowa with her husband, Tim, and Sparkle the rescue cat, namesake of Sparkle Abbey. In her day job she is the non-techie in the IT Department. Any spare time she spends reading and enjoying her sons and daughter-in-laws, and four grandchildren.

## Anita

**Anita Carter** is the "Abbey" half of Sparkle Abbey. She is a member of Sisters in Crime — Iowa, and a member of Mystery Writers of America, Romance Writers of America, Kiss of Death, the RWA Mystery Suspense chapter, and Sisters in Crime.

She grew up reading Trixie Belden, Nancy Drew and the Margo Mystery series by

Jerry B Jenkins (years before his popular Left Behind Series). Her family is grateful all the years of "fending for yourself" dinners of spaghetti and frozen pizza have finally paid off, even though they haven't exactly stopped.

In Anita's day job, she works for a staffing company. She also lives in Central Iowa with her husband and four children, son-in-law, grandchild and two rescue dogs, Chewy and Sophie.

The employees of Thorndike Press hope you have enjoyed this Large Print book. All our Thorndike, Wheeler, and Kennebec Large Print titles are designed for easy reading, and all our books are made to last. Other Thorndike Press Large Print books are available at your library, through selected bookstores, or directly from us.

For information about titles, please call:
    (800) 223-1244

or visit our Web site at:
    http://gale.cengage.com/thorndike

To share your comments, please write:
    Publisher
    Thorndike Press
    10 Water St., Suite 310
    Waterville, ME 04901